Josh Reynolds

This special trade paperback edition is
limited to 125 copies signed by the author.

Phileas Fogg
and the
War of Shadows

Phileas Fogg
and the
War of Shadows

Josh Reynolds

Meteor House

Phileas Fogg and the War of Shadows
by Josh Reynolds

Copyright © 2014 by The Philip J. Farmer Family Trust

Cover art and interior illustration copyright © 2014 by Amar Djouad

Meteor House

ISBN 978-0-9837461-6-4

First Edition Limited to
125 Signed Paperbacks & 125 Signed Hardcovers

For Sylvie

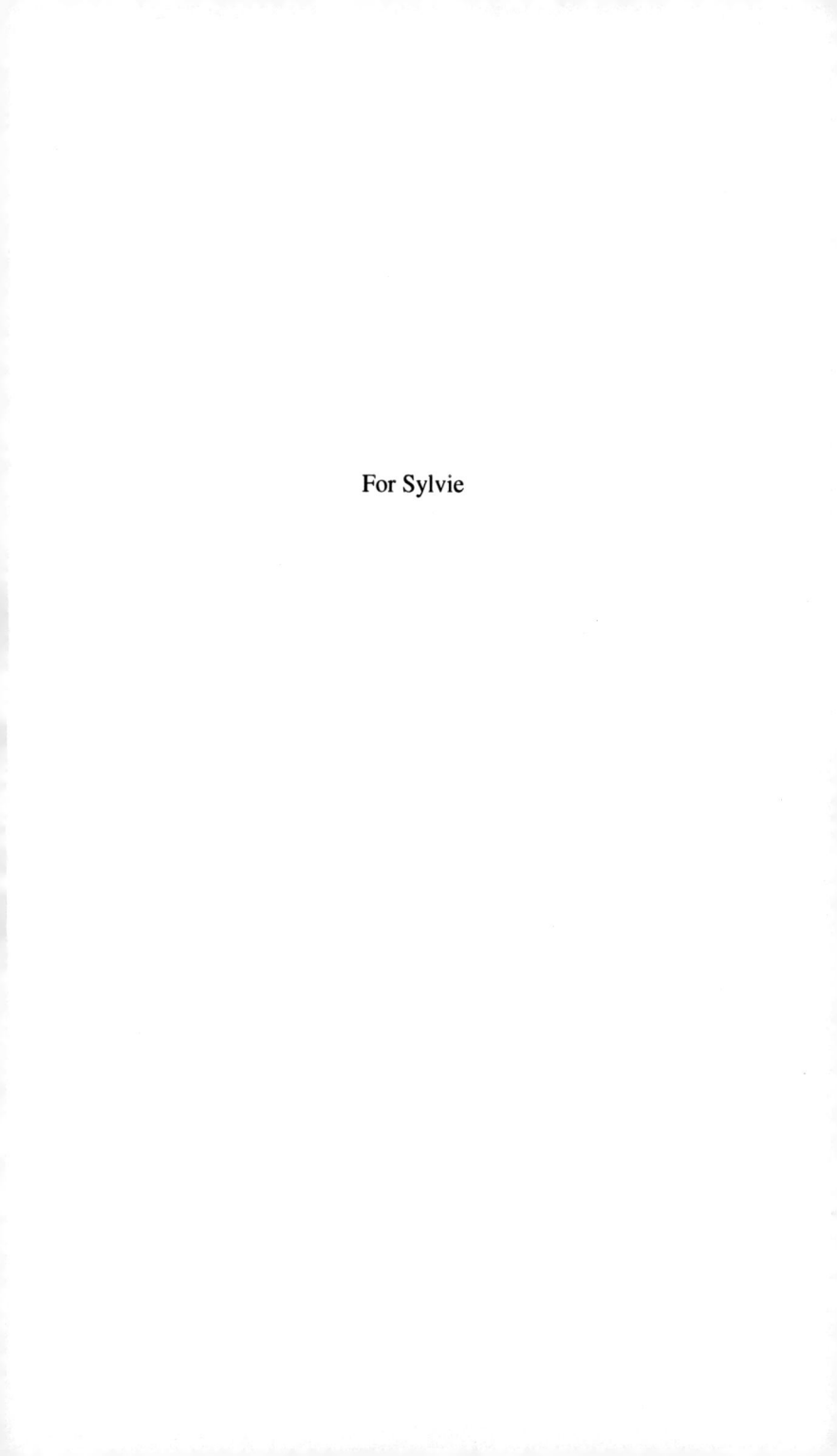

ACKNOWLEDGMENTS

Meteor House and the author would like to thank all of the following readers who preordered this limited edition novella and in so doing helped birth it into the world:

Ric Bretschneider, Peter Currane, Ray Riethmeier, Chuck Loridans, John Purdie, Jason Aiken, Michael R. Brown, Brad Kane, Christofer Nigro, Anthony R. Cardno, Rick Lai, Lisa Eckert, Robert R. Barrett, Peter Rubinstein, Patrick Miner, Ralph Carlson, Robert Craig, Paul Niedernhofer, Edward Lisic, Bill Wormstedt, Steve A. Heinrich, Peter Nuro, Anthony Kapolka, Daniel Ferranti, David Lars Chamberlain, Howard Smith, Mitch West, Wayne Turner, Ron Bachman, Carlos Martinho, Marty Kardon, Georgina Eloise Spiteri, Madeleine Lucy Spiteri, Steven Smith, Norris H. Hart, Dave Brzeski, Niall Gordon, Per-Olof Martinsson, Art Sippo, William Thom, David White, Joel Jenkins, Bryan Curtis, Denis Pike, Timothy Boyd, Enrico Barisione, Gary Rejsek, John LaFauci, Brian Johnson, Martin Gately, Bob Wayne, Karl von Hessel, Zacharias L. A. Nuninga, Greg Halliday, Andrew Friedenthal, Brian Berriman, Scott Turk, Sven-Marcus Björklund, David Joy, Paul F. Coyle, Jennifer Wright, Rev. Frank John Petrick,

Thomas Breslin, Charles C. Albritton III, Mark Edward Jordan, David Annandale, Robert Staszak, Kenneth Kessler, Alois Pirone, David Critchfield, Jack Connor, Steve Mattsson, Lucas Garrett, Dennis Hager, Michael Boner, Charles Prepolec, Paula Glaser, Grant Rybicki, Lee Fisher, David Rains, Patricia Wildman, Richard Lemon, Ronald Weston, Stephen Stirling, Willem Hettinga, Karl Schodrok, Richard Novak, A. J. Schuringa, Matthew Faso, Hans Kiesow, Rick Beaulieu, John Allen Small, James Karnesky, Jonathan Sweet, Lee Barrie, Colin Clynes, William Kerrigan, Mike Chomko, Herb Jacobi, David Soponski, Martin Brown, Baudette James Anderson, Bill Fannin, Thomas Von Malder, Theron Smith, Henry G. Franke III, Drake Maynard, Peter Sorensen, Brad Mengel, Thomas Bither, Stephen Kempton, Scott Stewart, C. Russell Stone, David E. Ray, Victor Litwin, Daniel Getz, Martin Jackson, Brenda & Ralph Reynolds, Jim Goddard, Bill Drummonds, Jeffrey Barbanell, Thomas Stephens, Stephen Iverson, Ward Orndoff, Joseph Anderson, John Streleckis, David Campo, Tarhan Kayihan, Ed Sanders, Royce Testa, David Cruces, James T. Allan, Douglas Daer, and Robert Lupton.

The publisher would also like to thank Win Scott Eckert and Sean Levin for continuity editing, Michael Croteau and Paul Spiteri for proofreading, Amar Djourd for capturing the look and feel of the story, Keith Howell for bringing the package together, and a big thanks to Christopher Paul Carey for bringing Meteor House and Josh Reynolds together in the first place.

Prologue

Fogg Hall
Fogg Shaw
Derbyshire
October 1975

Patricia,

I know it's not quite your birthday, but what's an auntie for, if not to spoil her dearest niece? You'll find your early birthday gift included with this missive—a quintet of leather-bound journals, very old, and very delicate. So be careful.

The journals are, as I'm sure you've discovered by now, written in a peculiar sort of cipher. I've seen similar codes before—need to know, before you ask—but these are outside of my expertise. And also quite indecipherable, at least by the boffins at the Service. I considered giving Jeperson's coterie a swipe at it, but the Diogenes Club isn't what it was, in better days.

Thus, it falls to you, dear heart, to unravel this conundrum. I know how you enjoy your little puzzles—that Xibumian affair for instance—so I thought you might fancy taking a crack at this particular riddle. Needless to say, loose lips and all that; we wouldn't want the wrong parties to take an interest.

But every good mystery needs a bit of context. The journals were found by an acquaintance of mine—no, you don't need to know who—while we were enjoying a quiet afternoon at the Fogg Shaw Barrow. And by quiet afternoon, I mean we were excavating a fairly odd little chamber, beneath the central stone formation. I can imagine the look on your face, Patricia, and I'll tell you what I told M . . . if my uncle can become an apiarist in his retirement, then I can engage in a bit of recreational archaeology.

Regardless, the chamber had been dug out once before, and given the char marks and other "observational detritus" as my father would have called it, likely by use of explosives, rather than honest toil. It was then subsequently filled in. The latter occurred after the journals were placed into a battered dispatch box (popular sort of time capsule for gentlemen of a certain age, no idea why) and then hidden in a narrow nook in the aforementioned chamber.

We only found the blasted thing by accident. The chamber itself is . . . well, I'll let you see it for yourself, the next time you visit. Suffice to say, those chaps at the Wilmarth Foundation are fairly salivating over the photographs I sent them. I've included copies of those photos, by the way.

Why someone (I suspect I know who, but I'll let you confirm or deny said suspicions before I mention any names) would hide these journals in such a place, I can't say, but I will admit that it does give me a bit of the old familiar tingle.

You see, while the code itself may be indecipherable, I recognize the handwriting. When I purchased Fogg Hall, I also purchased the contents of the house. And among those contents were the Savile Row papers that Sir Beowulf Clayton translated, copied, and passed on to our mutual friend, Philip José Farmer, not long ago.

PHILEAS FOGG AND THE WAR OF SHADOWS

You can probably see where I'm going with this, Patricia. And if not, you soon will. I have no doubt that you will decipher those journals the moment you turn your little gray cells to the task, as that obstreperous little Belgian was wont to say. Do write me, as soon as you've managed the first of them.

                        Dying of curiosity in Derbyshire,
                        V.

One

1889, Fogg Shaw Barrow

"This could not have occurred at a more inconvenient time," Phileas Fogg said tranquilly, as a stray bullet plucked his top hat from his head. He ran his gloved fingers across the irregular surface of the stone he and his companion had been forced to seek shelter behind only moments ago. The stone was long and wide and one of many which dotted the top of this particular moorland summit. It had been a hill fort, in some distant, savage time—Iron Age, he thought, or even earlier. It was old enough that its original name had been lost, and now it was simply known as the Fogg Shaw Barrow. Much like Fogg himself, it was a relic of a forgotten war. "I am certain that I was on the cusp of deciphering these markings."

"Yes, most inconvenient," Passepartout said. "Then, you'll forgive me, perhaps, Mr. Fogg, if I find that there is almost never a convenient time to be *shot at*!" His voice rose slightly, and he cowered as bullets plucked at the stone, and showered both he and Fogg with loose chips and dust.

"I beg to differ," Fogg said. He groped idly for his hat. "It can be most convenient, depending on the reason in question.

That said, I am most perturbed by this turn of events." His cool, calm gaze flickered across the stone and the ancient markings that covered it. He had been trying to translate them for months, certain that there was some meaning to them beyond the obvious primitive ritualism. Now, it seemed, his investigations would have to wait. "I assume you forgot to bring your pistol?"

Passepartout looked at him. "I don't own a pistol!"

"No? We will have to rectify that, once this matter is settled," Fogg said, as he examined his hat. The bullet had passed completely through it. With a sigh of disgust he sent it sailing away into the mist. He looked around. The standing stones were no fit place to make a stand, no matter their original purpose. They were contained within ragged outer walls that were six feet high, built of huge blocks of dark millstone grit, which surrounded the miniature labyrinth of oddly marked standing stones that spread outward in a slightly off-center fashion from a central barrow-mouth. It was, in many respects, the perfect place for an ambush.

He saw the shapes of several of their attackers moving through the early morning mist that yet clung thickly to the standing stones. Men, clad in black, and carrying firearms. An unusual encounter for rural Derbyshire, Fogg thought. The newcomers moved briskly, fanning out to surround them. None seemed to be armed with anything larger than a service revolver, for which he was thankful. One man with a rifle atop the tallest of the stones and his hat wouldn't have been the only thing perforated by a bullet.

"Who do you think they are?" Passepartout hissed. "Are they Capelleans?"

Fogg didn't reply. In truth, he was hesitant to make a guess. Though the great and secret war between the Eridaneans and their mortal enemies, the Capelleans, had been over for almost two decades, there were still hold-outs on either side who were determined to continue the conflict. Their attackers could well be Capellean or even Eridanean.

Fogg, though he didn't approve, understood—for most of his life, he had served the Eridanean cause, as had Passepartout. He had fought the enemies of his people from one side of the world to the other, only to discover in the end, they were not so different to himself. The last pure-blooded members of both races had perished in that eighty-day final skirmish which had begun, and ended, in the main hall of the Reform Club in 1872. As a consequence, the war which had so long been the central axis upon which his life and identity—as well as those of many others—revolved, had ended. There were some who, rather than feeling relief, as Passepartout or the repentant Capellean agent Fix did, refused to admit the war had ended.

"Their identity is of little concern at the moment, compared to our survival," Fogg said, finally. "I count five of them. An odd number, but survivable."

"You call this survivable?"

"They haven't shot us yet, have they?" Fogg said. Even as he said it, the thought occurred to him that perhaps they—whoever they were—didn't intend to. At the best of times, Fogg's mind was like clockwork, ticking along to its own steady rhythm. In times of stress, however, his thoughts became as quicksilver. Multiple possibilities surfaced, were examined, and discarded. His routine here, as it had been in London, was inviolate. Then, it had been a matter of camouflage. Here, it was a matter of habit. Regardless, he saw now he had allowed himself to become complacent. What had once protected him from prying eyes had now opened him up to an ambush.

But what was the purpose of it? Revenge, or something else? He brushed the thought aside. Such questions could wait until a more conducive moment. For now, he had other, more important considerations. Such as, was this sudden attack confined here, or were similar attacks occurring elsewhere on his estates. A face, containing brown eyes and framed by black hair, swam to the surface of his mind as he considered the latter and his reserve momentarily cracked. Ruthlessly, he forced his rising emotions back down, and sealed them away. He had been taught how to redirect his natural anxieties in order to retain his composure early on by his adopted father, an Eridanean agent of some distinction. There was a physical price to be paid for such an act, but it was worth it in the short term. A cool head and a calm demeanor were the best weapons he had at the moment.

"Aouda must be warned," he said. His wife, the daughter of a wealthy Bombay merchant and the widow of the Rajah of Bundelcund, as well as a former Eridanean agent, was as capable as Fogg himself. But there were his daughters to consider as well—Roxana and Suzanne. They were almost as gifted as their mother, but they lacked her training. Aouda would need help, if the estate were also under attack.

"And Sofia as well," Passepartout said fervently. After they had retired to the estates at the war's end, Passepartout had fallen for and married one of the local women. Pale-eyed and temperamental, Sofia was a match for the high-strung Frenchman, and Fogg had once amused himself by categorizing their many and multifarious arguments by decibel and length, though he'd refrained from sharing his findings with his friend.

"When I say go—run for the walls. Don't stop for anything," Fogg said softly.

Passepartout's eyes widened. "What about you?"

"In all likelihood, they are here for me," Fogg said. "Regardless, I intend to keep them occupied. Gather men from the estate, and come back as quickly as you can. Hopefully, I'll meet you on your way back. If not . . ." He fell silent. Passepartout paled.

"I should stay," he said.

"You are faster than I am. And as I said, they're likely here for me. You staying would serve no purpose," Fogg said. He hesitated. Then, he grabbed Passepartout's shoulder and gave it a quick squeeze. "We've been in tighter spots. Remember Bundelcund?"

Passepartout opened his mouth as if to speak, and then nodded. He grabbed Fogg's hand, but only for a moment. Then, he was gone, slithering quickly through the mist and stones. Fogg rose into a crouch and hefted his walking stick. He gave the stone a thwack and leapt over it, making no effort to hide his actions. He sprang for the nearest of the standing stones, striking them as he passed by. Voices were raised in sudden consternation, and shots tore through the mist. They'd seen him.

He moved quickly behind a stone. "Gentlemen," he said loudly, "I regret to inform you that you are trespassing on private property. The proper authorities will be alerted shortly. If I were you, I would give up this game of yours, whatever its purpose, and quietly leave. No attempt will be made to stop you." He waited. His assailants had fallen silent. Rock crunched under a sudden weight. Fogg saw something lunge towards him through the mist, and jerked his head aside. The man's fist struck the rock with a dull metallic sound, and Fogg realized his attacker was wearing brass knuckles. The man staggered, off balance from his fruitless attack. Fogg ducked and extended his cane between the man's legs, tripping him. Without pause, he gave the downed man a solid whack on the skull with his cane.

Quickly, Fogg dropped to his haunches and rolled his opponent over. He searched him, hunting for any clue as to who he was or who he might be working for, even as he kept his ear out for the others. The man was dressed in dark clothes that wouldn't have looked out of place in a Soho betting shop or on the wharves of Limehouse. He found nothing to identify either the man or his purpose. Fogg gave a hiss of disappointment and stood.

He heard a shout from somewhere behind him. They were coming after him now, as he'd hoped. He darted through the standing stones, leaving the unconscious man where he'd fallen, letting himself be seen, but only for a moment. He needed to keep them interested in him, and unaware of Passepartout's departure for as long as possible.

He pounded on, his breathing even, though his muscles burned from the unexpected activity. He had kept himself in shape, more out of habit than for any purpose. But his exertion wasn't the problem—there were only so many routes he could take before he'd run the maze in its entirety. The mist helped, but it would burn away before long, leaving him exposed. He slowed, and listened, one palm pressed flat to a standing stone. The mist and stones swallowed noise, and for a moment, all he could hear was the sound of his own breathing. Then, he heard the harsh rasp of another's breath, and the sound of boots pounding the soil.

Fogg slid about in a spume of mist, whisking the hidden blade from within his cane, and, without hesitation, spitted the gunman who rounded the corner of the stone he'd been sheltering behind. The dark-clad assassin gagged as the honed length of Damascus steel pierced his belly. Fogg thought, *That's two*, and gave the blade an efficient twist, as if he were coring an apple. He retracted the blade speedily and stooped to pick up the fallen man's pistol as the latter toppled forward with a fading whine. But Fogg was forced to abandon the weapon when a second would-be assassin leapt over the crumbling body as if it were no more impediment than a loose stone. A booted foot came down on the dropped pistol, and Fogg scrambled back.

This newcomer had a service revolver as well, and he fired at the already-running Fogg. The shot gouged a section out of the stone nearest Fogg's head as he moved and sprayed the air with particles of stone and grit. Fogg winced inwardly at the destruction being visited on the ancient site. As he dove between two standing stones, a second pursuer joined the first. Bullets plucked the dirt at his feet, sending him scrambling away. He knew they were herding him, but he couldn't tell the purpose. Had they set up a cross-fire ahead, somewhere amongst the stones? There was one man unaccounted for. If he was lurking somewhere up ahead, it was likely Passepartout had escaped, a thought which gave Fogg some small measure of relief.

Bullets bit at his coat and hummed past his ear. He struck a stone with his shoulder, rebounded and hurtled towards the heart of the site—a barrow-mouth, half-sunk in the soil of the hill. Fogg knew once he was in, there was little chance of getting out, but he saw no other option. Voices shouted excitedly behind him. He picked up the pace.

Even as he launched himself into the arguable safety of the barrow, he knew he'd made a mistake; he knew they'd been herding him towards this point all along. He bobbed to his feet and spun around, but too late. Something small and dark was flung in after him, and it hissed as it bounced across the rock. *Explosive*, he realized belatedly, as he whipped around and hurled himself farther into the barrow, seeking some form of safety from what was about to occur. Rocks tore at his clothes and the flesh beneath as he squirmed deeper into the sloping cavern, but he ignored the pain. Instead, he concentrated on the sound of the explosive as the hiss grew fainter and fainter, and on the face of his wife, which stood out in his mind's eye with a clarity that only imminent destruction provided.

Aouda, Fogg thought.

A moment later, the barrow was filled with thunder and fire, and then, finally, darkness.

Two

The silence of the barrow was broken sometime later by a ragged cough. Fogg blinked filth-caked eyelids and allowed himself a small groan, as he dragged his scattered thoughts into something resembling a cohesive whole. Instinctively, he took stock of his situation as well as he was able in the dark. Broken stones and loose soil covered him, and he felt as if he had been trodden on by an entire troop of Her Majesty's household cavalry. He had no way of telling how long it had been since the explosion. He didn't think he was hurt, at least not in any truly debilitating sense, which was something of a relief. His training afforded him the ability to switch off his pain receptors when necessary, but as with anything of that sort, there was a frightful cost in the long term for doing so.

The close air stank of sulfur and damp, and as he extricated himself from beneath his shroud of loose stones and dirt, he fumbled his handkerchief from his coat pocket and pressed it to his mouth and nose. He reached into his vest and retrieved a watch from his pocket. By feel, he gave the face a quick half-twist and was rewarded with a soft glow from its cracked face. The watch had a tiny solar battery of his own devising built into its case. Though the watch itself was damaged and no longer ticking, it was still fit for this purpose at least. The stored light wouldn't last forever, but if he were lucky, he would be out of the barrow before it faded. He extended the watch towards the wall behind him. A tumbled pile of rocks and a haze of still settling dust told the story there.

He'd been lucky the barrow walls had absorbed the brunt of the explosion. He'd managed to haul himself into a small heretofore undiscovered pocket of rock hidden at the back of the barrow in the nick of time, with the only casualty being his clothes, which had been badly ripped and torn. Light in hand, he rose to a stoop and peered about him. The pocket was barely large enough for him to get his feet under him, but the walls were smooth rock for the most part. Given the slope of the floor, he knew the pocket was located beneath the barrow. In fact, he judged it was quite likely the unseen aleph around which the standing stones had been set. The thought intrigued him. In all his months studying the Fogg Shaw Barrow, he'd never dreamed such a place existed.

His light caught dark markings on the walls. Crudely painted images—scenes ripped from prehistory—surrounded him. Strange shapes, unrecognizable to his eye, seemed to undulate in the soft glow cast by his watch. They were not human, and something about them sent a chill through his marrow. Before he could look too closely at them however, he heard the muffled sounds of digging. Instantly, he dismissed all thought of hidden chambers and strange markings and looked around for his cane.

There was every probability the unseen diggers were servants rousted from the estate by Passepartout. With his watch broken, Fogg had no sure way of telling how long he'd been semi-conscious in the dark—it could have been minutes, or hours. The rhythm of his internal calculations had been disrupted by the explosion. But it was just as likely it wasn't his people on the other side of the rocks, and his attackers were intent on making sure he was dead. Normally, Fogg felt such efficiency was to be commended. Here and now, however, he had the unpleasant sensation of being a rat in a trap.

He found no sign of his cane and gave a hiss of annoyance as he realized he'd likely lost it in the explosion. He was weaponless, and trapped. But far from helpless. Whoever was on the other side wouldn't expect him to be *compos mentis*; if he could seize the initiative, he might just stand a chance of seeing another nine hundred years of life.

As thin shafts of sunlight began to spear through the darkness, Fogg turned the light of his watch off and readied himself for whatever was coming next. When a heavy rock was hauled aside, and a waft of fresh air billowed into the pocket of stone, Fogg sprang for the newly made opening with a pantherish grace.

"Hup, back fools!" a voice cried out, as Fogg cleared the rubble and bounded to his feet with a tumbler's grace. Dust swirled about him in a cloud. Fogg looked around—a rough looking mob of men surrounded him, most holding the tools they'd used to dig him out of his makeshift tomb. They blinked in surprise. He couldn't tell whether they were friend or foe, and while they were still startled by his sudden appearance, he intended to put as much distance between them as possible. Discretion was the better part of valor in instances such as this.

Fogg turned to run, and immediately doubled over as a powerful blow caught him in the belly. "Oh no you don't," the same voice as earlier grunted. Wheezing, Fogg sank down to his knees. He looked up. The man who'd struck him was big, and his clothes were of a better quality than those of the men around him. "Looks like the tiger is out of the drain, hey?" he said, as he looked down at Fogg.

The face beneath the curled brim of the bowler hat he wore was familiar, though it had aged some since Fogg had last laid eyes on its owner. Cold, blue eyes peered out from under bushy eyebrows, and these, combined with the thin, long nose, heavy moustache and thick jaw combined to create a sensual yet ruthless image. The man radiated power as well as a certain debauched cynicism, and his lips twisted up into a grim smile.

"Well, I bet you never counted on seeing me again, hey Fogg?" Sebastian Moran said as he gazed down at Fogg. Fogg hadn't, but he saw no reason to admit as much.

"I do apologize—who are you?" Fogg inquired politely.

Moran's face flushed, and his lips peeled back from his teeth. His leg twitched, and Fogg knew Moran was contemplating giving him a kick. He decided not to give the other man a chance to indulge his sadism. Fogg, fully recovered now from Moran's blow, rose smoothly to his feet, and the other man stepped back with a frown. His coat was unbuttoned, and Fogg saw he had a cross-draw shoulder holster on. The latter held the blocky shape of a Mauser C96. Moran's gloved fingers brushed the semi-automatic pistol's grip, and for a moment, Fogg feared the other man was planning to gun him down where he stood. Then Moran grunted and snapped his fingers. Two of his men grabbed Fogg by the arms and they pinned his hands behind his back.

"It's your lucky day, Fogg. The chief doesn't want you topped," Moran said.

"Then what does he want?" Fogg said. He was careful to keep the shock he felt out of his voice. Moran's presence was surprising enough—but his mention of 'the chief' implied the involvement of another whom Fogg had hoped to have seen the last of. He'd first encountered Moran when the latter was in the service of the chief Capellean agent who called himself Nemo. The thought of Nemo sent a chill down Fogg's spine. Nemo had been the most vicious, if not the most effective, agent the Capelleans had. He was responsible for the deaths of many Eridaneans, and humans as well.

PHILEAS FOGG AND THE WAR OF SHADOWS

Fogg had come into direct and open conflict with Nemo in 1872, during his attempt to recover an enemy distorter from the Rajah of Bundelcund, a former Capellean agent and would-be world-beater. Nemo too had been attempting to reclaim the device from the treacherous rajah, and he and Fogg had clashed again and again over the course of Fogg's infamous eighty-day journey around the world.

"That's for Himself to say, ain't it?" Moran said. "Let's go."

Fogg was escorted down from the barrow by Moran's men, who tossed him into the back of a horse-drawn wagon he recognized as belonging to his estate. The horses were his as well, and he felt a flare of annoyance. Moran joined him in the back of the wagon, and sat silently as it trundled back towards Fogg Hall, situated in the heart of the Derbyshire countryside.

Fogg sat up as they neared their destination. The manor house looked much as he had left it that morning, save for the preponderance of armed men who now loitered on his grounds. They were a hard-faced lot of ruffians, none of them local, he suspected.

"You killed one, if you were wondering," Moran said suddenly.

"I wasn't," Fogg said.

"Cool one, aren't you?" Fogg looked at him. Moran smiled nastily. "Gutted him as sweetly as I've ever seen." He made a swift motion across his belly with his thumb. "Very pretty," he added.

"Was he one of yours?" Fogg asked.

"What makes you think that?" Moran said, and fell silent. He said nothing more until they'd reached the manor house. Fogg was manhandled out of the wagon by Moran's men, and frog-marched through the front doors of his own home, like a defeated commander being taken to meet the man who'd scaled his walls and thrown open his gates. Moran led the way, marching smartly to some inner drumbeat. Fogg took the opportunity to look around. There were no signs of violence, for which he was thankful. Whatever had happened, had happened quickly and, hopefully, bloodlessly.

Aouda's face swam before his eyes once again. The cold, alien portion of his intellect said it was unlikely she had been harmed—she was too valuable for that. The other, larger side of him felt a sharp pang of worry for her and his children. He worried for Passepartout as well. He'd seen no sign of him at the barrow . . . had he been captured by Moran and his men? Or had something else happened to him. Fogg forced the thought aside, and fought to maintain his composure.

Moran led him through the house to his study. Fogg wanted to laugh. Of course. Where else would Nemo choose to meet him? "He's waiting in there," Moran said as his men opened the door. He planted his hand between Fogg's shoulderblades and gave him a shove, propelling him through the door and into his study. Fogg maintained his balance, but only just. Moran was strong; something to keep in mind for future encounters, he thought as Moran came into the room behind him. Fogg straightened the hang of his coat and brushed grime from his sleeve as he surveyed his study. Everything seemed to be in order. Nothing appeared to have been taken, or moved. But something had been added.

On his desk sat a silver tea set from downstairs, and the grim shape of the Webley service revolver Fogg normally kept in his desk drawer. His wingback chair was occupied by a slender shape, clad in a stiff black suit several years out of fashion. As Fogg made a show of checking his cuff links, the latter took a sip from a cup.

"Hello, Fogg," Nemo said, as he set his cup down on the saucer he held. "Retirement agrees with you. You look much the same as when we last . . . spoke."

Fogg gazed at the hateful, almost reptilian, features of the one man he'd thought never to see sitting behind his desk, in his study, in his house. The years since their last encounter had not been kind to Nemo. He'd developed a slight, oscillating twitch which only added to the air of snakelike malevolence his stoop-shouldered, bald headed frame radiated.

Once, he had been a giant, in stature and build—now he was a wizened thing, shrunken and reduced. His hands trembled slightly as he set the cup and saucer aside. Fogg had, during their earlier encounters, come to believe Nemo had developed a fault in his neural conditioning while in service to his race's goals. Like Fogg, Nemo could almost certainly seal off his traumas, fears, and shocks to better deal with them at a later date. Fogg suspected, however, it was that last bit that had become unduly troublesome for his old enemy, and had resulted in a premature physical wasting to go with whatever unseen mental degradation was likely to have occurred.

Like all Capelleans—and all Eridaneans, for that matter—Nemo had partaken of the alien elixir which made him the next best thing to immortal; but, whatever malady had him in its clutches seemed to have wrung that immortality from him. In Fogg's cool estimation, made the instant between sight and recognition, the man before him had only a few years left, if that.

"Byronesque, yes, that is the term, I believe," Nemo continued. "A Byron, before dissolution and death wrung him dry. You are a credit to your people." He pushed himself to his feet. "Leave us, Moran," he said. Moran hesitated. "I said leave us," Nemo snapped. He sliced the air with the edge of his hand for emphasis. It was still a powerful looking hand, for all that it twitched like a dying insect. Moran grunted, nodded, and left the study, closing the door behind him. Nemo stared at the door for a moment, and then turned his attention back to Fogg. "Sit, Eridanean," he said.

"Seeing as it's my study, I believe I'll stand," Fogg said.

He cast his gaze about the room, letting it linger on the bookshelf, where several volumes had been plucked from their proper places and set atop their fellows. When he had left that morning, all of his books had been in their proper places. It could have been Nemo's handiwork, but he doubted it.

Nemo shrugged. "Sit or stand, as long as you listen do as it pleases you." He went to the window and stared out, his thin hands clasped behind his back. "Those men who attacked you were not in my employ. Nor were they agents of the Capelleans."

Fogg said nothing. Nemo's fingers twitched like the legs of an enormous spider. "They were not Eridaneans either. They are, to mangle a phrase, new pieces on an old board." He turned. "You understand." It wasn't a question, or, at least, Fogg did not take it as such. Though his appearance had changed, Nemo was a pedantic as ever.

"I do," Fogg said. "Why were they here?"

"They were looking for Eridaneans. Or Capelleans; they aren't choosy," Nemo said. "Someone has become aware of us—of our people. How, I do not know, though I intend to find out and punish those responsible." He twitched, like a cat dreaming of mice. "Several of my former comrades-in-arms have gone missing over the course of the past few months. I make it a point to keep tabs on the survivors of the Great War, as, I'm sure, you yourself do."

"I do not," Fogg said, softly. In truth, he had considered it, if only so that he knew what creatures like Nemo or Moran were getting up to. But he had decided against it. He was no longer a soldier or strategist. Nemo gave a raspy laugh.

"You are lying. Eridaneans always lie."

"Why are you here, if you weren't behind the attack, Nemo?" Fogg asked. He was careful not to let his annoyance show in his voice.

"I call myself Moriarty now, Fogg. Professor James Moriarty, at your service," Nemo—Moriarty—said, as he inclined his head and spread his hands in a theatrical gesture. "I have not been to sea in some years. Not since you snatched a hard-won victory from my hands with your Eridanean tricks." He made a face. "I confine myself to the choppy seas of academia now."

"Moriarty then. Answer my question. Where is my wife? Where are my daughters? Where is my manservant?" Fogg demanded. Fogg was certain the man before him was as dangerous as ever, whatever his name, and despite his apparent weakness.

"The latter is not here, sadly. The former are in my care, for which I expect some modicum of acknowledgement, if not gratitude." Moriarty cocked his head. "I saved them, you see. I came to save you."

Fogg hesitated. "What?"

"Through certain... sources, I became aware that this new Enemy's sights had become set on you. Thus, I made preparations to travel to Derbyshire with a suitable force of men in order to prevent another of our... fraternity, from falling into their hands. As I said, I come as your savior, not as your enemy."

"Now who's lying?"

Moriarty expelled another raspy laugh. "Would that I were, Fogg. Would that I were lying, would that I had my hand about your throat in this moment, and the freedom to... simply... *squeeze.*" Moriarty began to twitch more violently than before, as if he were overcome with the force of whatever emotion he was feeling. His lips peeled back from his teeth, and Fogg was reminded of a serpent, readying itself to strike. The moment passed, and Moriarty was once more his own master. He relaxed and shook his head. "But I am constrained by necessity." He looked at Fogg.

"You see, I need you, Fogg. I need your help."

Three

Fogg blinked. "My help," he said. The thought was almost unimaginable, not only because Moriarty had tried to kill him on numerous occasions. Moriarty's ego was such that the very idea of him requiring or asking for help was an impossibility. His eyes flickered to the revolver. Moriarty, as if reading his mind, crossed the desk and hefted the weapon. He cracked it open and emptied the cartridges onto the desk with a negligent flip of his wrist. He slapped the barrel and cylinder back into place and extended it, grip first, to Fogg. "Will this put your mind at ease?"

"My equilibrium is undisturbed, thank you," Fogg said.

"Ha," Moriarty sneered. "More lies. But it is of no importance. Is the fact that I require aid so inconceivable? Surely, the reason is obvious, even to the limited intellect of an Eridanean."

"I'd be insulted if I still considered myself such," Fogg said. "We are human, Moriarty. The last pure-blooded member of the Eridanean race perished some time ago. As did the last pure Capellean. You will recall the latter, given that you were there at the time."

Moriarty flinched. He gestured sharply. "And so? Are we not still heirs to their legacy?"

"And seemingly the targets of their enemies," Fogg said.

"Not enemies . . . Enemy. Singular," Moriarty said. He raised a finger like a school-teacher. "We—Eridaneans and Capelleans both—are opposed by a singular mind, driven by a desire as yet unknown. He has captured our people, tortured them, and robbed them of their secrets."

Fogg paused, struck by a terrifying thought. "What secrets?" he asked softly.

Moriarty cocked his head. "The distorters," he said. The distorters—matter transmitters of immense capacity and range—were among the greatest of the devices the Eridaneans and Capelleans had passed down through the generations of war. Designed to look like watches of great size and intricate design, the distorters had been a weapon much sought after by both sides, when the ability to perfectly produce them had been lost. Indeed, the retrieval of a distorter had been at the heart of Fogg's famous eighty-day global circumnavigation. Passepartout possessed one, and Fogg the other, as well as the schematics for their design.

After the Eighty-Day Affair had been concluded, he had placed both devices out of reach of would-be possessors, and the schematics he possessed had been burned. It wasn't inconceivable that other schematics existed, but the machinery required to construct the devices was still several generations from being developed by human scientists. An Eridanean or Capellean might possess the capacity to create a workable distorter from current technology, but it would be a chancy thing, one few members of either race would be willing to attempt.

A human, however, might be willing to gamble everything on the possibility of acquiring a method of instantaneous transport. Fogg could call to mind any number of petty tyrants or criminally inclined individuals who might risk such a thing; creatures like the sinister Dr. Nikola or subversive organizations like the Si-Fan would dare much to possess a working distorter.

Fogg closed his eyes as the dreadful possibilities washed over him. He cursed himself for not keeping better tabs on his former comrades in arms. If Moriarty were correct, and they were being hunted, then Fogg had committed a grievous error in judgment. "You are certain?" he asked, after a moment.

"I am."

"And you know this how?"

Moriarty smiled crookedly. "I have my ways."

Fogg frowned. "Why did you come? There's no love lost between us."

"I came to deny the Enemy a resource," Moriarty spat. He tapped his brow. "We two are the greatest remaining minds of our disparate organizations. To allow you to fall into the hands of the Enemy would be folly." His eyes narrowed to slits. "I considered simply killing you, but to do so would be a waste and a risk. The war has ceased, but it is not done while those who still remember it live. Your death by my hand would start the conflict all over again. That is something I cannot afford at the moment." He fell silent.

"And," Fogg prodded, after a moment.

Moriarty's head oscillated and he turned away. "And I require your mind, Fogg. I have the army, but no commander to lead them." He twitched and glanced over one bony shoulder. "You will be my marshal, my Bessieres, to Moran's Murat," he said. "I require a ratiocinator to balance my killer."

"What are you talking about?"

"I have located the Enemy's lair. I have devised a stratagem to remove him from the board. But I lack the time to devote to it at present. My empire is beset by other enemies."

"You never did have a problem irritating the wrong people," Fogg said.

Moriarty whipped around to glare at him. His hands quivered and clenched. Fogg watched him, unperturbed. "You are a fool," Moriarty snarled. "I come to you in good faith, I come to your aid, and this is how you repay me?"

"Spare me the aggrieved histrionics, I implore you," Fogg said. He didn't flinch from Moriarty's display. "You didn't come to aid me, you came to harm your enemy, whoever he is. You admitted as much just now. You say you have other enemies—I expect that you do, for you are without a doubt one of the most callous, appalling creatures on this planet. You make enemies the way a gambler racks up debt, Moriarty. Why should I help you in this war of yours? Why should I trust your word on any of this?"

Moriarty looked at him for a moment. Then, he smiled. Fogg's blood ran cold, and the answer came to him in a flash. "Aouda," he said.

Moriarty inclined his head. "And your daughters. They are quite the lovely pair. A credit to you and their mother, in my humble opinion." He grasped the air, his fingers curling into his palm like the talons of some predatory bird. "I own their lives, Fogg."

"And Passepartout? You said he wasn't here. I assume that means you are not holding him captive as well." Fogg calculated the odds of his friend having escaped, and found it too close to call one way or another. Passepartout had been one of the most cunning operatives that Fogg's people had possessed. But it had been years since he had had to put those abilities to the test.

Moriarty sniffed. "To the best of my knowledge, the Enemy has him. That is another factor to add to your calculations as to my trustworthiness. Your servant will be tortured like the rest, for whatever information he has, unless you can find and rescue him. I will help you do so, as in doing that, I help myself."

PHILEAS FOGG AND THE WAR OF SHADOWS

"I wish to see my wife and children, before I agree to anything," Fogg said, after a moment. Moriarty twitched, as if in surprise.

"No," he said.

"No?" Fogg wasn't surprised. He had expected the demand to be denied, at least initially. But there was something in Moriarty's manner that implied the denial wasn't wholly out of spite, or out of a desire to make his enemy squirm.

"No," Moriarty said. "I am in charge here, Eridanean. I will not have you passing secret messages to your slattern and spawn. I know the tricks you Eridaneans devised, and I do not trust you not to attempt to turn this situation to your advantage."

"As a Capellean would, you mean?"

"Exactly," Moriarty said, and gave a harsh laugh.

"But you aren't a Capellean anymore; nor am I an Eridanean. We are only Englishmen, and it is not proper that you should deny me a last look at my wife," Fogg said.

Moriarty clapped his hands together. "Oh, I have missed you, Fogg. I have missed the game and the war. The Great Plan was so close to fruition, and then you swept aside the game board and ruined it all, and for what? To retire to a life of rural drudge?"

"The word you're looking for is 'idyll,'" Fogg said.

Moriarty waved Fogg's words away as if they were bothersome gnats. "Frankly, you should be thanking me. I am not simply the savior of your body, but your mind as well."

"Oh?"

"Don't play coy, Fogg. Your edge has dulled here, in this *idyll*," Moriarty said, almost spitting the last word. He tapped his egg-shaped skull. "Your mind languishes in chains of routine. You are bored."

There was a certain uncomfortable truth to that, Fogg had to admit, even if only to himself. When the war had ended, and he had sought the quiet of the countryside, he had thought to find some sense of inner peace. But a lifetime spent training for and then participating in a vast conspiratorial conflict had engendered in him a restlessness he had not anticipated.

He could feel a spark of anticipation, warring with his concern for Aouda and his children, and Passepartout as well. Moriarty wouldn't harm them, if, indeed, he even had them. His hesitancy to allow Fogg to even see his wife had aroused certain suspicions. But it wasn't merely Moriarty's reticence that had alerted Fogg to a possible deception. He and Aouda had developed numerous contingencies for every possible situation—from a renewal of hostilities to a global conflict. Each contingency had its own signal, known only to Aouda and himself. Even Passepartout was ignorant of them, not because Fogg mistrusted his friend, but because he knew the optimum number for secrecy was two.

The removal and placement of certain titles on his bookshelf—the organization of which he had memorized—constituted a warning from Aouda. Fogg suspected she had been alerted to Moriarty's arrival and taken the girls and gone into hiding, leaving the warning for him, in case Moriarty had chosen to ambush him.

There was also the very real possibility Moriarty himself had displaced the books in question. He could have done so either out of boredom, or because he'd calculated the odds of Fogg and Aouda having a way of speaking to one another without talking or even seeing one another, and theorized as to the manner and parts of that process.

Fogg looked at Moriarty. Even with the twitch, it was almost impossible to tell what the other man might be thinking. Moriarty was as intelligent as he was malignant. He was a cancer at the heart of whatever society he was a part of, but a *thinking* one. His plan was not as simple as he described, of that much Fogg was sure. Treachery was second nature to Moriarty. He had betrayed the Rajah of Bundelcund, the crew of the *Nautilus*, and the Capelleans themselves without hesitation. There was no reason to think he didn't intend the same for Fogg.

But the facts were plain, no matter the messenger. Both Eridaneans and Capelleans were in danger. Passepartout was gone. If Moriarty assumed he had been taken, Fogg was forced to admit the likelihood of that possibility was great. Which, in turn, meant that he had no choice. All of this went through Fogg's mind in seconds. Moriarty watched him, and Fogg fancied the criminal was making his own calculations, trying to gauge the latter's response. Fogg took a breath. "Where is this enemy, then?"

Moriarty relaxed. "Paris," he said simply.

"You have made arrangements?" Fogg found himself slipping easily back into the role of agent. Moriarty inclined his head.

"Of course. I had no doubt as to your decision." He smiled. "Moran will accompany you. He will act as my right hand, and you will act as my left," Moriarty said. "You will run the Enemy to ground and then my *shikari* will take his pelt." Moriarty clenched his fist and smiled cruelly. "He kills men the way a person might kill a fly, my pet colonel—a reflex action. A twitch of the wrist. I have high hopes for him."

"And if I fail?" Fogg said.

"Then nothing of what happens after will likely matter to you," Moriarty said. "Rest assured Fogg, the Enemy is as much your foe as mine. And unless we make common cause, we will both fall."

FOUR

"Care for a game of cards, Fogg?" Moran said, shuffling the deck with impressive dexterity. Fogg twitched his newspaper aside and eyed the other man. They had taken passage aboard the *Calais/Douvres*—a steel paddle-steamer, owned by the London, Chatham and Dover Railway Company, which plied the ferry route from Dover to Calais.

The trip from Derbyshire to Dover had been accomplished aboard Moriarty's private train. The latter had taken the opportunity to lecture Fogg at length on all that was known of the Enemy. He had compiled quite the dossier on his as-yet-unidentified foe. Fogg was duly impressed, though he didn't say so. Even so, the dossier and the accompanying discussion, had been disturbing in the extreme.

A number of recent events in the past two years, according to Moriarty's information, had been either capitalized on or caused by agents of the Enemy, as a cover for the kidnap of an Eridanean or Capellean agent. The brief abortive mutiny in Dufile, India; the Johnstown Flood, in western Pennsylvania; the great fire which had ravaged Seattle on the sixth of June; the Armagh rail disaster in the north of Ireland. The list was thorough. Fogg had been moderately surprised to see that the by-now-infamous killings which had viciously etched the name of Whitechapel into the British consciousness were not mentioned. To him, the ritualistic barbarity of the killings had seemed an obvious smokescreen for something else, but Moriarty had dismissed the idea.

Regardless, it swiftly became evident the Enemy had some inkling of the Great Plan. Certain members of both races had been kidnapped, both in England as well as on the Continent. The operatives of both races had been spread across the globe. Even Fogg, as highly placed as he had been, hadn't known where all of his fellow Eridaneans were. He didn't even know how *many* of them there were, Moriarty's assurances of dwindling numbers aside. Indeed, though he recognized several of the names on the list of kidnapped individuals, he wasn't entirely certain they were even Eridanean.

The bodies of those so taken had shown up here and there, in bits and pieces. That they had been tortured was obvious. Whoever the Enemy was, he wasn't squeamish, and he seemed to have learned the art of questioning from Oriental teachers, given the evidence. The notion stirred the faint undercurrent of worry that flowed beneath Fogg's train of thought and his fear for Passepartout grew as Moriarty went on at length about the barbarity of the foe they faced.

Moran, the train's only other passenger, had paid little attention to Moriarty's sermon, ostensibly having heard it all before. Instead, he'd busied himself packing all manner of strange devices and unpleasant implements, broken down into seemingly innocuous components. Fogg was certain Moran's luggage contained at least two weapons, including one of the deadly airguns designed by the blind gunsmith, Von Herder. What the other was, he couldn't say, though he intended to find out, at the first opportunity.

Moran sat opposite Fogg, and as he fiddled with his cards, the latter caught sight of the Mauser holstered beneath his arm. Fogg hadn't brought his pistol, reasoning that unless Paris had changed since his last visit, there were likely firearms aplenty should he require one. Instead, he'd contented himself with a replacement for the cane he'd lost at the barrow. The slim length of lacquered wood currently leaning against his knee contained a finely crafted blade of Damascus steel. The weapon was light, springy, and lethally sharp, much like its owner.

He and Moran sat at one of the many tables which had been set up beneath a tent on the aft deck of the *Calais/Douvres*, just behind the second of the paddle-steamer's twin smokestacks. The clanking, rhythmic rumble of the bank of paddle wheels that occupied the space between the smokestacks, and separated the prow of the ferry from the aft section, filled the air, making conversation difficult. There weren't many passengers. They had taken the last ferry from Dover, and between the weather and the late hour, they had the passenger section mostly to themselves. Fogg pulled out his watch—a replacement for the one broken in the explosion at the barrow—and flipped it open. They would be in Calais in half an hour, at most.

Upon reaching Calais, they were to take the first available train to Paris, where Moriarty's continental agents would make contact with them. He looked forward to seeing Calais once more, though they'd hardly have time to enjoy it. Paris, as well. Fogg found the elegant chaos of the City of Lights alluring, despite his preference for routine and schedule. When he and Aouda had undertaken a much more sedate trip across Europe in order to celebrate their nuptials, they had spent several delightful weeks in Paris. There, Passepartout had introduced Fogg to his associate, Jules Verne, the man who would write a highly fictionalized account of their circumnavigation of the globe.

At their first meeting, Verne's wit and enthusiasm had

charmed both Fogg and Aouda. He was smart, literate, and amusing. Verne was apparently a town councilor in Amiens, now, which struck Fogg as both fortunate for Amiens and unfortunate for everyone else. He clicked his watch shut. As he placed the watch back into his vest pocket, he caught sight of a young man in a dark overcoat watching them, from several tables over. The man looked away as Fogg caught sight of him. Fogg frowned.

"Did you hear me, Fogg?" Moran said, shuffling the cards.

"I'm sorry, I was reading about the dockworkers' strike," Fogg said, pushing aside thoughts of Verne, Paris, and young men with suspicious faces. "They're asking for an increase in wage," he added.

"Bloody socialists," Moran said. "They should give them a kick up the arse, if you ask me." He shuffled the cards again. "In India, we knew how to deal with shirkers."

"I'm certain," Fogg said. He folded the paper and set it aside. "I'm assuming you're not in favor of New Unionism, then."

"I believe in the two party system," Moran said cheerfully, "the masters and the slaves." He laughed uproariously and Fogg smiled thinly.

"Which one are you?" he said.

Moran's laughter was cut short. He frowned for a moment, and then met Fogg's gaze and grinned slowly. "I'm English, ain't I? It should be obvious, even to a fool like you."

"Do you really believe that?"

Moran made a face. "Do you want to play or don't you? I've heard you're a dab hand with the cards."

"You don't play whist, I suppose," Fogg said.

"Need four for that," Moran grunted.

"Ask me again when you've made two friends."

Moran set the pack of cards down and tapped it with his

finger. "Careful, Fogg. I might just take it into my mind to shoot you in the head and tell Himself the Enemy did it."

"He'd know you were lying, and have you killed for it," Fogg said.

Moran chuckled. "Probably," he said. He leaned back in his chair. "It might still be worth it, just to see the look on your face and his."

Fogg inclined his head. "One finds one's pleasures where they must, I suppose."

Moran leaned forward and planted an elbow on the table. "Ever been to Paris, Fogg?"

"Yes," Fogg said.

"So have I," Moran said. "Himself has quite the network there. Lots of pickpockets and doxies and apaches all pay a tithe to the great man." He pulled a small, ornate snuffbox from within his coat and flipped it open. He took a pinch, and returned the box to his pocket without offering any to Fogg, who was less insulted than he was amused.

"You admire him," Fogg said, looking out at the water.

"I admire organization," Moran said. "I'm not a Capellean, you know."

"I know," Fogg said. He hadn't, but saw no reason to acknowledge such. In truth, he knew little of Moran, save he was, or had been, a soldier of some distinction before he'd become too hot for the military to hold him.

"Not Eridanean either," Moran went on. "I was a mercenary in your little war. An Englishman abroad, a stranger in a strange land. Oh, I knew all about the Great Plan, for Himself has never met a subject that he didn't pontificate on at length. I know about that dashed elixir as well, though not a single drop has ever passed my lips, more's the pity. That's why I was there that night, in 1872, with Vandeleur and the others. 'Human minds,' he liked to say then, 'human minds are what's needed for this war, Moran.'" He laughed. "Now that it's just us humans, he's a bit wistful for the old gang, I think." He rubbed his nose and sniffed.

"I understand," Fogg said. And he did. Secrets weighed on the soul and the mind like anchors. The larger the secret, the heavier the anchor. It helped to have someone to share it with. Every year, the remaining members of the two races drifted further apart. With the Great Plan abandoned and the war ended, there was no reason to keep to the old ways, the codes and secret gestures. Indeed, it was better for everyone if such things were forgotten. If mankind ever learned there were two alien species among them, however human-seeming, there would be trouble. Fogg had had more than one nightmare about it. Nightmares that seemed, unfortunately, to be now coming true.

"I doubt it," Moran said. "You've got your brown-skinned bride and your froggy manservant to confide in. All Himself has is me, and old Tiger Jack is many things, but an ordained confessor ain't one." He picked up the deck of cards and began laying them out as if to play solitaire. "If I thought I could get away with it, I'd sell the story for more money than I could waste in a lifetime." He looked at Fogg slyly. "But Himself would have my guts for garters before the words left my lips."

"He wouldn't be the only one," Fogg said.

"No? I rather had the impression that you'd left it all behind," Moran said. He snapped cards down atop the discrete piles forming in front of him.

"Some responsibilities cannot be laid aside so easily."

Moran smirked. "Never had that problem, myself."

"No, I do not expect that you do," Fogg said smoothly. He stood. "I'm going to take in the sea air. Do not feel that you have to join me."

"Oh, but I do," Moran said. "I'm not letting you out of my sight, Fogg. I don't trust you as far as I could throw you."

PHILEAS FOGG AND THE WAR OF SHADOWS

"The feeling is mutual," Fogg said. He didn't wait for Moran to gather up his cards. He strode across the deck, towards the paddle wheels. The *Calais/Douvres* was quite large, as Channel-going vessels went. It was certified to carry over a thousand passengers, had a crew complement of fifty-nine and could travel at 18 knots, according to official records. Fogg thought the latter was perhaps a judicious estimation. By his own calculations, the vessel was traveling at just under sixteen knots, though that might have been due to the weather.

The deck close to the paddle wheels was mostly empty, which wasn't surprising, given the time of night and the chill wind rolling across the waters of the Channel, as well as the noise. Fogg and Moran were alone, and they crossed the deck in silence, the latter with his hands thrust in his pockets. Fogg stopped by the rail and took a deep breath. Ahead of him, he could see the lights of Calais. From behind him, he could feel the pulse of the wheels.

He wondered where Aouda was. He was certain now that Moriarty didn't have her. On the trip to Dover, he had had more time to study his onetime enemy up close than ever before, even during their time aboard the *Nautilus* together. Moriarty was, by turns, arrogant, supercilious, and pedantic. He was a man certain of his own superiority, and with the wit and cunning to back it up. But he was also beset by worries.

Moriarty, Fogg realized, wove plans like spiderwebs, surprisingly strong, but simultaneously fragile and vulnerable to errant, unconsidered factors. Apparently, one of those factors—a certain London-based consulting detective of whom Fogg knew little and cared even less—had graduated from nuisance to obstacle, and it was on this threat that the majority of Moriarty's attention was focused, even as he outlined for Fogg the danger which faced their peoples. That one man could be considered so dangerous by the former Capellean chief was either a sign of his capabilities or an example of the degradation of Moriarty's faculties. Fogg suspected it was a combination of both. This opponent, whom Moriarty referred to only as 'the detective,' was in the process of dismantling the criminal empire Moriarty had built in the years since the war's end. Such a direct threat was impossible for Moriarty to ignore, even with the activities of the Enemy menacing him from afar.

No, Moriarty didn't have Aouda. If he had, he would have shown her, or their daughters, to Fogg, in an effort to impose his will upon his former rival. Of that much, Fogg was now confident. He felt a sense of relief at the thought, tempered by his ongoing concern for Passepartout. If the Enemy were indeed after the secret of the distorters, the men who'd attacked them at the barrow might not have been after him, as he'd initially assumed. Passepartout had been given the duty of carrying and using a distorter during the Eighty-Day Affair, and there were a number of Eridaneans who'd known that, besides Fogg and his immediate superiors.

At the thought of Passepartout, he felt a brief stirring of guilt. He wondered if the Enemy truly had him, or if that too was another gambit on the part of Moriarty. He strongly suspected the latter, mostly because he was still, as yet, uncertain he could trust Moriarty's identification of his attackers. Given the evidence, and his own experience with the man formerly known as Nemo, he could say only that Passepartout's current fate was up for debate. The thought did not lend itself to maintaining his composure.

In truth, it was becoming more and more difficult for Fogg to control his emotions. His once-rigid schedule had been disrupted by family and friends in ways not even the war could have matched. The children alone had been more disruptive than any scheme of Moriarty's, and even though they were now on the path to adulthood, they were still as disruptive and anxiety-inducing as ever.

PHILEAS FOGG AND THE WAR OF SHADOWS

Fogg let his gaze drift across the deck. He caught sight of the same young man he'd noticed before, in the dark overcoat, standing near the smokestack, a halo of cigarette smoke now rising over his head. He could not be sure, but he thought the man was watching them. He was younger by a decade or two than both Fogg and Moran; barely out of his teens, in fact. A young man, perhaps embarking on the first leg of a trip abroad he thought. But something about the fellow pricked at Fogg. There was something about the set of his face, and the look in his eyes, that elicited an atavistic shudder.

As he watched, the young man pulled a tarnished watch out of his coat and flipped it open with a curious gesture that was eerily familiar. A chill swept through him. He was suddenly reminded of what Moriarty had revealed about the Enemy's purpose. Could it be—? Was the man watching them carrying a distorter? That disturbing thought was uppermost in his mind when the first thunderous clang shook the sky and sea.

FIVE

The sound, when it came, was so unexpected that even Fogg, normally as phlegmatic as a stone, was startled. He shuddered as the great clanging rolled over the Channel. Moran clapped his hands to his ears and cursed. Gulls streaked into the air, shrieking raucously. The horribly familiar sound battered at their ears, and Fogg felt the vibrations echo painfully in his skull. "Moran," he said tersely, as he hefted his cane. He looked around. The young man had vanished.

"I know," Moran grunted. His hand dipped into his coat. Before Fogg could react, Moran drew his pistol and spun, aiming directly at him. Fogg froze, but only for a moment. Even as Moran snarled, "Get down!" he dove to the deck. The Mauser in Moran's hand spat and a black-clad body was snatched from the air and sent whirling out over the water. Fogg bobbed to his feet and interposed his cane between Moran's broad back and the blade that had been stabbing towards it.

The knife's wielder was clad in loose black clothing, and his face was hidden behind a formfitting hood. He wore a pistol holstered on his hip, and had a bandolier of thin bladed knives slung across his chest. As he stepped back, he drew one of the latter. Blade in either hand, he swept silently towards Fogg. Fogg blocked one blow and then another as his assailant drove him backwards. He heard Moran curse and the Mauser spoke again as several more black shapes glided towards them across the deck.

Fogg batted aside a knife that sought his belly and made a smooth fencer's lunge with his cane, striking his opponent in the throat. The man staggered and Fogg ducked low and struck the former's ankles, knocking his feet out from under him. As his enemy fell, Fogg reached out and snagged the other man's pistol, yanking it from its holster. He turned and saw another assassin hurtling towards Moran from behind. Fogg hesitated for a millisecond, and then fired, catching the black-clad killer in the back. The man fell with a muffled cry. Moran glanced back and gave a grunt of what might have been thanks.

"This enemy of Moriarty's is wasting no time," Fogg said, as he and Moran went back to back. He hefted the pistol. "How did he know we were coming?"

"Same way Himself knew the Enemy was in Paris, I expect," Moran drawled. "This shadow war of theirs has been going on for a few years now. This is just the last big push."

Fogg grimaced. Bereft of the Eridaneans, Moriarty had found a new partner to play his favorite game with. He wondered how much of this was about the kidnapped members of their races, and how much of it was simply Moriarty entertaining himself. He shook the thought aside. Moriarty's true motivations could wait—right now, he needed to concentrate on the enemies in front of him.

The black-clad assassins had surrounded them. But the clanging and the sound of gunfire, however muted by the crash of the paddle wheel, had alerted the few passengers and the crew to the fact that something was afoot. There were only four of the killers left, and as several members of the crew rushed towards them, the assassins sought what cover they could find on the deck, upending tables and drawing their pistols, cracking off shots at this new threat. Moran shoved Fogg towards the smokestack. "Where's the boy?" Moran snarled.

"Boy?" Fogg said.

"That whelp in the black coat," Moran said, peering around. "You saw him, Fogg. I know you did." The assassins engaged the crew, and the sound of pistols rang out. "He's a sneaky one, but not sneaky enough to avoid Tiger Jack's eye."

"You've seen him before?"

Moran gave a sharp bark of laughter. "You could say that," he said. "Himself didn't tell you how he knew about the enemy's interest in those blasted distorters, did he?"

"He didn't mention it, no," Fogg said. Moriarty had refused to tell him how he knew what the Enemy was after. Fogg had begun to suspect that, given Moriarty's own fixation on divining the secrets of the ancient technology, he had simply projected his obsessions onto his foe. But given the all-too familiar clanging sound they'd heard, Fogg was forced to admit Moriarty was correct. His mind whirled—how had the Enemy gotten his hands on such a weapon, much less both parts? Distorters required both a transmitter and a receiver to function. Had someone he'd taken revealed the location of a heretofore unknown pair of distorters? Or had he learned how to construct them for himself? Neither thought was especially pleasant. A thought struck him—could the boy be the Enemy? "Who is he?" Fogg demanded.

"The boy? No idea," Moran said. "I think—Ha! There he is!" He rose to his feet and fired his Mauser over the top of the paddle wheels, towards the gantry opposite them. Fogg looked and saw the man in the black coat duck low. There was something in his hand. A dark, small device. An image of the explosive that had trapped him in the barrow flashed across his mind.

"He's going to sink the ferry," Fogg shouted.

Moran whipped around to look at him. "What?"

Fogg didn't bother to repeat himself. There was no time. He only had a few moments to act. He tossed aside his cane and lunged for the iron ladder attached to the side of the smokestack. Swinging himself up, he leveled his pistol. The man in the black coat saw him, but reacted too slowly. Fogg's shot grazed his shoulder, and the explosive device went flying from his grip. The device struck the paddle wheel, and Fogg flinched, waiting for an explosion that never came. The device hadn't been armed!

Without regard for the red patch marring the sleeve of his coat, the young man leapt up onto the rail and vaulted off onto the top of the paddle wheel. The device had become lodged into the scoop of the wheel and he seemed to be intent on reclaiming it, or at the very least, activating it. He scrambled awkwardly across the wheel, towards the explosive. Fogg took aim, but when he pulled the trigger, the revolver gave a sad click. He pulled the trigger again, to no avail, and then tossed the weapon aside in disgust.

A complex sequence of calculations speared through Fogg's mind, as he gauged the distance. With the briefest of prayers, he swung out from the ladder and dropped towards the rotating paddle wheels below. He landed where he'd hoped, but even so, the spume of water and churned foam made it nearly impossible to keep his balance. His shoes slipped and slid on the edge of the wheel, and even as he stood, he was nearly pulled off his feet to a watery doom. The man in the black coat saw him, and redoubled his efforts to snatch the explosive from where it sat.

Fogg could hear Moran cursing from behind him, but he focused on the lean shape of his enemy. The young man strained for the device, but as Fogg drew close, he bobbed to his feet with a grace that put Fogg in mind of a serpent readying itself to strike. The man's black gaze pinned Fogg in place, but only for a moment. Fogg lunged for the device, but a length of blade appeared suddenly in his opponent's hand and he was forced to slide back as it nearly severed his jugular.

"Who are you?" Fogg spat. He'd been taught to spar by the best pugilists his adopted father, Sir Heraclitus Fogg, could hire, but the young man moved less like a fighter than an animal.

"Who am I? Nobody," the young man said splashing towards him, blade in hand.

"And yet obviously, somebody. Why are you here?" Fogg said, spreading his hands. He was confident he could block the younger man's blow, though it would cost him blood to do so. The young man smiled cruelly. There was no passion in that smile, no fire.

"To spread terror," he said. He came at Fogg in a rush, gliding across the rolling surface of the paddle wheel like a dancer. If Fogg had been any other man, without the iron control instilled in him by the teachings of the Eridaneans, the smile, the words, the attack, all of it would have caused him to hesitate. Instead, he met his opponent's rush. He swatted aside the blade with the flat of his palm, even as he drove the stiffened fingers of his other hand into his opponent's chest, just beneath his sternum. The young man gasped at the unexpected force behind the blow, and Fogg managed to catch him by the back of his coat as he staggered. He drove his knee up into the young man's belly. The knife clattered away and was lost in the agitated water below.

As he shoved his dazed opponent aside, Fogg caught sight of the watch chain bouncing on the outside of the latter's coat pocket. Instinctively, Fogg reached out to snatch it. If it *was* a distorter, he needed to gain possession of it, as soon as possible. But the young man wasn't quite as dazed as he'd thought, and Fogg suddenly found himself toppling backwards as his foot was yanked out from under him. His head struck the hard edge of the paddle and the world spun around him in a nauseating fashion. He looked down, and saw the water churning only a few feet from his head.

Still dazed from the fall, he clawed desperately at the surface of the wheel, trying to prevent himself from tumbling into the water. The edges of the wheel thudded against his back as he tried to push himself up. He saw his opponent climbing the wheel, one arm reaching between the paddles. With a final burst of effort, Fogg thrust himself up and flung himself at his opponent. He caught him by the back of his coat and, with a surge of desperation-induced strength, slung the young man back and away, sending him rolling away down the wheel. The young man's face twisted in a moment of panic just before Fogg lost sight of him. Then he was swallowed up by the foaming waters.

Fogg snatched the explosive from where it was trapped. Quickly, his long fingers scrabbled across it. The device was a mishmash of Eridanean and human technology, cobbled together with an artisan's flair. He had used similar explosives—often hidden in watches—in his previous life. Perched on the wheel, Fogg swiftly deactivated the device, turning stems and unwinding tiny cranks. Cradling it to his chest, he scrambled off the paddle wheel, sopping wet and soaked to the bone. As he clambered over the rail, Moran was there, hauling him back onto the deck. "Where'd the little blighter go? I lost sight of him," he said, as Fogg pushed him away.

"He went under. I believe he—" Fogg began, but was interrupted by the nine thunders of the distorter. He clapped a hand to his head as the air vibrated with the clangor of the device for long minutes and then faded.

"He survived, the little rat," Moran said, his disappointment obvious. He'd holstered his pistol. The crew and passengers were in an uproar. Bullet holes and bloody smears decorated the deck here and there. The assassins had vanished. Even the dead ones were gone, which was something of a disappointment. Fogg had hoped to examine one of the bodies. He settled for studying the explosive. It had been constructed with more care than such a device normally required. The designer had had an artist's touch, adding purely decorative flourishes to the casing and structure. Nonetheless, the device was compact and sturdy. He was reminded again of his watches.

The attack, while not successful, had served to crystallize several of Fogg's growing suspicions. If the Enemy possessed distorter technology, as he so obviously did, why hadn't he used it at the barrow? The assassins had not been dressed like those who'd attacked him at the barrow. Nor had they seemed to have any interest in capturing him. Too, their coordination, their weaponry, all of it spoke as to a different methodology. But the explosive was similar. Then, anyone who had participated in the war would know how to construct a similar device.

He was certain, now, the attack at Fogg Shaw Barrow had been an elaborate ruse, designed to provoke him. Moriarty would not be above such tricks, but what was the purpose? Was Moriarty's position truly so tenuous that he required an agent with similar training to himself to act in his name? Why not simply acquire the services of any one of a dozen Capelleans he was likely at least on speaking terms with?

The only answer Fogg could come up with was less than heartening. Moriarty had, it seemed, merely delayed his long-desired vengeance on the man he saw as his rival. And if, in the process, he could kill two birds with one stone, well, that would suit the man formerly known as Captain Nemo just fine.

Moran pointed to the explosive. "Best hand that over,

Fogg. Wouldn't want the authorities to spot it. They might think you're a bomb-throwing anarchist, and then where would we be, eh?"

Fogg bobbed his head. "You are quite correct, Colonel." He turned and, before Moran could stop him, let the device tumble from his hand to be caught by the paddle wheel and swept under water. As Moran cursed, Fogg watched the explosive vanish.

The Enemy had a mind, then, that was certain. A renegade, perhaps, like the late, unlamented Rajah of Bundelcund, or even Moriarty himself. Or, more disturbingly, a human capable of reconstructing alien technology without the benefit of the accumulated teachings of the Eridanean and Capellean peoples.

Unless that was the whole purpose of the kidnappings—the two sides of the war had had more technologies available to them than simply distorters, but as the knowledge of how to repair and maintain those technologies became increasingly rare, they had fallen out of use. By Fogg's day, only the elixir, the distorters and certain explosives had been still used regularly. That didn't mean an enterprising mind might not make use of such things, if they were to stumble across them.

He looked towards the approaching lights of Calais, and couldn't help but wonder what awaited them in Paris. Regardless of his reasons, Moriarty had, perhaps, done the right thing in contacting him, Fogg thought.

He was now convinced the Enemy, whoever they were, was a threat to the remaining members of both races. And Fogg, despite his protestations to the contrary, had never truly stopped thinking of himself as an Eridanean. As he'd told Moran, some responsibilities could not be laid aside so easily.

"Once more, unto the breach," Fogg murmured.

Six

The port authorities in Calais had been most interested in the events aboard the *Calais/Douvres*, but both Fogg and Moran had experience in avoiding inquisitive investigators. Too, Fogg had no doubt Moriarty's reach was long enough to have smoothed their path somewhat. Their passports were stamped without fuss and they swiftly slipped through the grasp of the police and were aboard an early train bound for Paris. It would take them no more than a day, to reach their destination. Moriarty's schedule was still intact.

Fogg spent most of the journey perusing French newspapers for any hint or sign of untoward occurrences that might hint at the Enemy's plans. Moran, as ever, amused himself. The Colonel made a less pleasant companion than Passepartout, Fogg felt, but Moran wasn't accompanying him because of his social skills.

The attack on the *Calais/Douvres* was would likely be reported as an attempt at political sabotage by anarchists. When in doubt, Fogg knew, one could always blame anarchists.

As the train sped towards Paris, Fogg mused on the possibility of another attack. The assault on the ferry had had all the earmarks of an impulsive gambit. True, the explosive would have obscured all sign that anything untoward had occurred, but it still felt wrong somehow. How had they known he and Moran would be on the ferry? Information was as deadly a weapon as any blade or bullet, and he had the distinct and unpleasant sensation he was being driven into battle less well-armed than he'd like.

He thought again of the young man who'd been carrying the distorter. He'd have to have followed them from Dover, and perhaps longer than that. Fogg neatly folded the paper he'd been reading. "Did you recognize him?"

Moran glanced up from his game. They were seated in the dining car, and had been for nearly two hours. By Fogg's estimation, they were still three hours out from Paris, regardless of what the rail schedule said. Moran picked up his fifth scotch of the hour and knocked it back. "Him who," he said.

"Our young friend with the distorter," Fogg said serenely. He looked around the car, taking in the faces of those around them One, a striking young girl, barely out of her teens, met his gaze and blew him a cheeky kiss. Fogg looked away as she rose from her seat and left the car. He gave the matter no more thought. The French were, after all, a flirtatious people. "You've seen him before. And you were not entirely surprised to spot him on the ferry. Who is he?" he asked.

"No clue who he is," Moran said. "I know what he calls himself. And what he is."

"Then what is he?"

Moran grunted. "Besides bothersome? He's one of the Enemy's creatures. He's named Gurn, I think. Or that's what he's called, at any rate."

"How do you know?"

Moran stared at him for a moment. "How do you think I know, dash it? He's tried to kill me more than once. And the rest of us—all of Moriarty's errand boys. He nearly pushed old Fred Porlock off a platform at King's Cross. He tried to gut me in Bordeaux last year. He hung a second story man of my acquaintance from a bell clapper in St. Michaels after opening his throat with a straight razor." Moran smiled faintly. "The boy, whoever he is, is precocious, I'll say that for him. A keen talent for murder most foul."

"How do you know he isn't the Enemy?"

Moran snorted and looked back down at his cards. "Because he's a savage little blighter, but he's not a thinker. Himself is certain there's a cooler, wiser head aiming the little rat in the right direction. And I don't disagree. I've known many a throat-slitter, and they're not big thinkers, by and large."

"Masters and slaves," Fogg murmured.

Moran looked at him. "Ha! Yes, exactly. He's somebody's dogsbody, right enough."

Fogg sat back. "Why pick a fight with Moriarty?"

"What do you mean?"

"I mean, what started the war?"

"Himself told you," Moran said, laying down a card.

"Moriarty has never been loyal to any creed save his own. Even his own masters feared him. So you'll forgive me if I don't take his word at face value," Fogg said. "He may have noticed the pattern, but I'd wager it's something else that interests him."

"You're free to wager what you wish," Moran said, setting down another card.

"It's the distorters, isn't it?"

Moran said nothing.

Fogg sat back. "I never understood why he was so obsessed with them. There are quieter methods of assassination, and as far as housebreaking goes, you'd have to have someone inside anyway. They are merely tools, and fiddly ones at that."

Moran concentrated on his cards. Fogg sighed and stood. "I'm going back to our compartment. Enjoy your game."

"I always do," Moran said, without looking up.

Fogg made his way into the next car, his mind awhirl with possibilities. If Moriarty was after the distorters, things were starting to make more sense. The man formerly known as Nemo had scoured the world for the distorters once, even going so far as to infiltrate the citadel of the Rajah of Bundelcund in an effort to purloin the latter's device, ostensibly at the behest of the Capelleans. Fogg knew better, however. He'd clashed with Moriarty often enough to know just what sort of man the other was, and that his goals were never so simple as they seemed at first glance. The question was, which of the dozens of possible goals he'd identified since first laying eyes on Moriarty in his study was the latter pursuing?

Still caught up in his calculations, Fogg paused in the corridor and took a moment to admire the view flashing past. He leaned forward, as something caught his eye. The door to the compartment he and Moran shared was reflected in the glass, and he could see a shape within. Fogg tensed, but gave no sign he'd noticed anything amiss. Perhaps the attack on the *Calais/Douvres* hadn't been as impulsive as he'd thought. He'd left his cane in the compartment, but he was hardly helpless. Whoever was in there hadn't yet noticed him, he thought. He readied himself, and then darted for the door to the compartment, flinging it open with a loud cry.

Fogg had hoped to startle whoever was in the compartment, but he hadn't expected him to immediately dart for the door opposite. With a crash, the slim, slight figure smashed the outside door of the compartment open, allowing a rush of cold air to billow into the room, even as he swung out onto the outside of the train with a commendable display of acrobatic skill, and scurried up the side, towards the roof. Fogg was so startled that he didn't react immediately. The compartment was a shambles. Neither he nor Moran had brought much in the way of luggage, for obvious reasons, but what they had brought had been opened and quite obviously rifled through. With a curse, he kicked the outside door shut and lunged back out of the compartment, startling a matron and her attendant, who let loose a string of Gallic oaths as Fogg loped down the corridor, his head angled to catch the sound of his quarry above. He could just make out the thump of his feet above the rumble of the train.

Whoever it was, was heading for the rear of the train. Fogg ran through the cars, dodging passengers and trying his best to keep pace. While his quarry had a clearer route, Fogg didn't have to worry about keeping his balance on the roof of a moving train. When he reached the baggage compartment, he brushed past the attendant and made his way out onto the rear of the train. He could tell from the lack of thumps above, that he had outpaced them, whoever they were. Wind rushed past him as he clambered out onto the railing and reached to grab a handhold on the roof. Despite his headlong flight, he hadn't made his pursuit wholly on instinct. Whoever had been in the compartment had been looking for something, and he intended to find out what.

He'd been atop a moving train more than once, and while it wasn't an experience he relished, he couldn't help but feel a slight pulse of anticipation as he hauled himself up. He had missed this, he realized. Moriarty had been correct, at least in this regard. While he had not missed the uncertainty and fear that went with such escapades, he had missed something about them. The wind whipped around him, hammering at him from all sides as he rose to his feet, arms slightly spread to help maintain his balance.

A thin, dark shape was winnowing towards him. He speculated, as he set himself in his quarry's path, on their reason for running in this direction. Were they intending to slip back into the train through the baggage car? Or was there some other reason?

He got his answer a moment later, as something caught

his eye. He looked up and only just managed to restrain an exclamation of surprise as he saw a hot air balloon sweeping down towards him, along the length of the train. The balloon itself had been painted the color of the sky overhead, and the basket was a pale color, allowing for it to move mostly unseen, unless one noted the shadow, as Fogg had. And, as he watched, the crew of the balloon let down a rope ladder.

Fogg turned his attention back to his quarry, who'd stopped upon sighting him. He recognized the young woman from the dining car almost immediately. She had changed out of her dress into a black outfit that resembled a set of full body tights. Even her hair was hidden beneath a tight hood that left only the pale oval of her face uncovered. She was younger than he'd first thought, but not frightened at all. She watched him warily, with the alert poise of an alley cat, interrupted on its nightly prowl.

He started towards her slowly, but stopped when she plucked a thin knife from the sheath strapped to her thigh. "You are quick, monsieur," she shouted, in French. "Or are you simply eager to have another kiss from me?"

"I am quite happily married, mademoiselle," Fogg yelled in reply, in the same language. "But I would like a word with you as to why you were in my compartment." He started forward again. The movement of the train made it hard to keep his balance. "Who are you?" he shouted. "Who do you work for?"

"No one and nobody," the girl said.

"Then why were you going through my things?"

"Who says I was going through yours, hey?" she shouted back.

The thought gave him pause. Moran had his own luggage. There was no telling what was in it. Moriarty had sent them to destroy his Enemy, after all, and Moran was his killer. Fogg had suspected Moran was carrying a larger arsenal than simply his Mauser, but he'd avoided asking the question. He'd intended to snoop himself, while Moran was occupied in the dining car. The girl had simply beaten him to it.

"*Touché.* Perhaps you'd care to explain further," Fogg said, drawing closer. She was little older than his daughters, he saw. A pang went through him at the thought.

"No, I am afraid that I simply must dash, monsieur. Places to go, people to see," the girl said. She laughed and stretched out an arm towards the rope ladder that was hurtling towards her as the train passed beneath the hovering balloon. Fogg hurried towards her as fast as he was able, hoping he could tackle her before she caught hold of the ladder.

The ladder smacked into her palm even as he reached her. Her knife slashed out, and Fogg reared back, guarding his face with his forearms. The blade whipped lightly across his coat sleeves, sending buttons flying. Then the girl was shimmying up the ladder. Fogg reacted quickly. He latched on and was almost immediately yanked off of his feet. His heart lurched in his chest as he suddenly found himself dangling above the moving train.

From above him came a yell, and his heels struck the roof of the train. As he'd hoped, his weight had pulled the balloon off course. Quickly, he wrapped his arms through the rungs of the ladder, so that he wouldn't be easily dislodged. If he could force them to descend, he might be able to gain the advantage.

It wasn't to be, however. A padded sole smacked into the side of his head. Stars burst behind his eyes and he swung around to the other side of the ladder as the girl descended quickly, her blade clutched between her teeth. She held onto the ladder like an acrobat and, with a nigh-impossible twist of her hips, she raised her legs and thrust both of them through a gap in the ladder in order to catch Fogg in the side with a kick that would have done a mule proud.

Fogg's knees struck the roof of the train car, but he didn't let go of the ladder. The girl spun about until she was hanging upside down above him. She grabbed his chin in a surprisingly strong grip and retrieved her knife. Fogg released the ladder and wrestled awkwardly with her. "Who are you?" he gasped, "Who are you working for?"

Her only answer was a shriek and a vicious slash that sent him reeling back. His foot became tangled in the ladder as he stumbled and the balloon bobbed upwards again, dragging him off his feet and dropping him onto his back. His shoulders struck the roof of the train. As he dangled, momentarily helpless, his watch tumbled from his vest and bounced in front of his face. The girl's eyes widened and she immediately began to slither down towards him, curses spattering from her lips.

Fogg's eyes flickered from her to the watch as he realized his weight was still anchoring the balloon, at least for the moment. She launched herself at him, her previous playfulness discarded and replaced by a ferocity that would have startled him, had he not been in firm control of his reactions. But even as she drove her blade towards him, she was clawing for his watch.

He shoved her grasping hand away with his knee and slapped his palms together, trapping her blade as it darted for his face, and tried to twist it out of her grasp. The bobbing of the balloon made it difficult, however. His shoulders rose and fell with the balloon, and she had better leverage. The girl strained forward, and her blade slowly slid through his grip towards his throat.

Then, suddenly, her weight was yanked from him. A moment later, the familiar *crack-crack-crack* of Moran's pistol reached his ears. He twisted around and saw his traveling companion crouched on the rear of the car, firing up at the balloon's occupants. Fogg took the opportunity to untangle himself. Then he sought out the girl. She was laying near the edge of the roof, her black outfit stained red along one arm.

Fogg saw she had no way of holding onto the train, and she was slowly being dragged towards the edge. She rolled over onto her back as he approached.

"Take my hand," he shouted.

She gazed at him blearily. Then, with a startling serenity, she blew him a kiss and allowed herself to be pulled off the train. Fogg lunged, but was too late. She was gone in an instant. He turned as a sandbag struck the roof. Moran cursed and dodged a second, nearly joining the girl in oblivion. The balloon was rising away. There was no sign that Moran's shooting had been in any way effective.

"Fogg, are you all right?" Moran bellowed, staggering towards him against the wind. "I caught sight of that blasted gas bag out of the dining compartment window, and decided to investigate."

"The girl—she fell," Fogg said.

"Good," Moran grunted. He watched the balloon recede into the distance. "Little witch threw half of my luggage out of the compartment window. All of my toys are gone, save Sister Abigail, here." Moran patted his Mauser. He looked at Fogg. "Our tiger is clever, Fogg. He's killed our beaters and driven off our pack animals."

Fogg said nothing. He shook himself and said, "Let's get back inside. We'll be arriving in Paris soon."

Seven

Thunder rumbled somewhere behind the dark clouds which choked the skies over Paris, and rain, steadily growing in intensity, tumbled down to patter against the stretched canvas surfaces of hurriedly erected awnings and tents, as well as those of hastily deployed umbrellas.

Despite the bothersome weather, Fogg couldn't help but marvel at the sheer titanic spectacle of the wrought iron edifice Gustave Eiffel had designed, and which now served as the entrance arch to the Exposition Universelle. The Eiffel Tower rose up around and above him, piercing the sky. It was a magnificent achievement, both in terms of design and engineering. Far above, he could see the doll-like shapes of workmen hard at their labors.

The Tower wasn't yet finished, though visitors could ascend to the second floor observation platform, if they wished. Men had worked through the night before the grand opening of the Exposition several months before in order to ensure it was safe for visitors. Fogg found himself wishing he had but a few moments free to climb the edifice. He pushed the thought aside to concentrate on the matter at hand.

The incident on the train had receded to the rearmost

portions of his psyche, to be dealt with at a later date. Whatever her purpose, whoever she had been acting for, the girl was gone and he was left with more questions than answers. He'd hoped to hear a clanging, as he had with the young man aboard the ferry, but no such sound had been forthcoming.

Fogg had been trained as a soldier, and he viewed such losses with a soldier's eye. Killing an enemy in combat was one thing, but letting them die for no good reason—that irked him. Moran had shot her as surely and as coolly as he might have potted a game-bird. He'd saved Fogg's life, but whether that had been his intention was still up for debate. He seemed to feel little concern either way. For a man lacking entirely in Eridanean neural conditioning, Moran was putting on a good imitation. Fogg was beginning to think his traveling companion, besides being a barbarous danger addict, was also a thankfully rare example of one of Julius Koch's congenital psychopaths.

It was no wonder Moriarty kept the Colonel close to hand, or that he had brought him into the inner circles of the Great Plan. Such a callous creature was the perfect blunt instrument for a mind like Moriarty's to employ.

As they joined the vast crowd which was slowly filing into the Exposition in the shadow of the Eiffel Tower, Fogg took note of their surroundings. The central portion of the Exposition had been constructed on the Champ de Mars, but it had expanded to include much of the area. In effect, it was a small city within a city. There would be thousands of people inside.

Moran groused irritably as they moved through the crush of eager visitors. They'd arrived via the small, three kilometer train line that carried visitors to the Exposition, and had been caught in the crowd since embarking. Fogg, knowing full well the dangers of such crowds, kept one hand on his billfold in his coat, and the other on his hat. He allowed Moran to lead the way, trusting in the other man to clear them a path with the sheer stream of muttered expletives emerging rapid fire from his lips, if not his bulk.

Moran was still angry over the loss of his baggage, and Fogg was still puzzled. Surely there were easier ways of divesting them of their gear. A baggage handler, or a ticket attendant could have done the same thing, and with less chance of arousing suspicion. Unless, of course, Moran's arsenal had only been one of several goals.

He thought about the girl, and how she'd fixated on his watch. Could that be it? But why—unless someone thought it was something other than what it was. And why would they suspect that, unless someone had told them. His previous assumption of Passepartout's escape became suddenly more nebulous. Could the Enemy indeed have his friend? And if so, what else had Passepartout told him?

As Moran bulled ahead, Fogg kept watch on the sea of faces that swirled about them like ripples in the waters of the Seine. If the Enemy had been keeping tabs on Moriarty, as he suspected, it was likely there were agents of both factions in this private war present even now. Or even more than that—Moriarty had made no bones about the number of enemies he'd acquired in the years since Fogg has seen him last.

Rival organizations and individuals with names like Quartz, Kramm, Nikola, and Bozzo-Corona dueled with Moriarty through intermediaries and proxies. The Si-Fan and the Red Hand, the Golden Chrysanthemum and the Black Coats were all nipping at the heels of Moriarty's British operations. The last of those was the preeminent criminal organization in France, and while Moriarty claimed to have applied his deadly mathematics to controlling their organization from within, Fogg suspected that was wishful thinking on his part. Still, it begged the question—could his Enemy be some part of that organization out to stifle Moriarty's overweening ambitions in their crib? Or perhaps it was some other, unknown threat?

The latter hadn't seemed to have occurred to Moriarty, and Fogg hadn't seen fit to share it. He'd considered asking Moran, but doubted the Colonel had anything pertinent to add to his own theories.

The more Fogg considered the war he'd found himself drawn into, the more he realized the quarrel between the Eridaneans and the Capelleans had likely been but one of hundreds of similar secret, conspiratorial conflicts that raged even now across the globe. Initially, he'd thought many of these had merely been outgrowths of the Great Plan, like barnacles growing on the hull of a vessel as it traveled. But now, the more he considered it, the more he was coming to believe the Great Plan was merely one of many, and that his people were merely one element at play in some great game whose rules and limits he had yet to divine.

And that thought was the most disturbing of all. It was as if the ground beneath his feet had turned to sand. Nothing was certain anymore. Once, the sides had been clear, and the players evident, but now . . . now he saw that had never been the case.

The strange cave paintings he'd seen briefly in the barrow had continued to haunt him, if only intermittently throughout the journey from Derbyshire. They had depicted a war, he now thought, but not a war he was familiar with. How long had Earth been a battleground? It was obvious his people were not, their assertions to the contrary, the first alien species to visit Earth, or even to settle upon it. How many of those ancient colonists had brought with them their own conflicts? How many of those conflicts continued to this day, in secret? He shook the thought aside, and moved closer to Moran. They were almost inside the Exposition grounds, and the crowd was picking up speed. "Where are we going?" he asked quietly.

Moran didn't look at him. "The Hall of Machines, or, as

the froggies say, *Galerie des machines*," he said. "It's just up ahead. First stop in this gaudy carnival."

"How appropriate," Fogg murmured. The Hall was a pavilion located in the Grenelle District, at the foot of the Champ de Mars. Crafted from iron, glass, and steel, it was supposedly the largest vaulted building in the world, big enough to contain fifteen thousand horses in the ground floor and their riders in the upper galleries without being crowded, though how they'd arrived at that precise number, Fogg couldn't imagine.

"Bloody annoying is what it is. Why they couldn't meet us in the French section, where the Imperial Diamond is being held, I don't know," Moran said. "I'd like to get my hands on that."

"Moriarty didn't send you to pilfer a gem," Fogg said. Moran grunted, but said nothing. "Where are we meeting them?"

"Just past the main hall, on the moving bridges." Moran pointed ahead of them.

Fogg frowned. "Which one? There are several, if I recall correctly."

Moran shrugged. "It'll be one of them. We'll just ride them all until they find us."

"I can see why Moriarty's organization is under siege, if that's the sort of thing that passes for strategy in it," Fogg said. Moran laughed.

They followed the crowd into the central dome. It was a high, vaulted space that echoed loudly with the voices of the crowd, magnifying and amplifying the voices until the noise rivaled that of the storm outside. The floor of the dome was occupied by two large sculptures. One showed a triumphant archangel standing over the broken coils of a dragon, and preparing to deliver the death-blow with a long spear. Behind the plinth it occupied was the second, much larger sculpture of some triumphant heroine, goddess, or muse, mounted on a mighty chariot pulled by four great horses. There were benches arranged between them, and behind them was the entrance to the gallery itself. Two sets of stairs, one to either side of the dome, led up to the upper gallery where the moving bridges chuffed and chugged their way across the hall beyond, carrying people to and fro.

Moran grunted suddenly. "Tigers in the long grass."

Fogg didn't need to ask him what he meant. A crowd of this size, trapped in such a narrow space as the entrance hall, was as much a dangerous environment as any shadow-filled back alley in Limehouse.

Fogg's cane snapped down, deflecting the knife stroke that would have otherwise taken Moran in the kidney. Moran spun with a snarl, and drove one meaty fist across the face of his would-be killer. Before he could slump, Moran grabbed him by his lapels. He'd struck him so quickly, and so forcefully, that no one in the crowd around them seemed to have noticed. Fogg examined him quickly. He was dressed like a day laborer, but he had the muscle tone of an athlete and the complexion of a night owl. He scanned the floor for the knife, but couldn't see it. "He isn't one of ours," Moran growled. He didn't bother to thank Fogg this time, an oversight for which Fogg forgave him. They had other problems to worry about.

"Neither, I'd wager, are they," Fogg said, gesturing with his cane. More men were winnowing through the crowd towards them, faces set. The hall was crowded, and the ambush had been perfectly timed. If the knife-man hadn't made his move a half-second too soon, Fogg had no doubt he and Moran would have been dead before they realized it.

Moran reached for his Mauser, and then cursed. "My pistol is gone," he muttered. "Some light-fingered froggy has had it while we were pushing through to get in here, I'd wager."

"Perhaps it's for the best—somehow, I doubt we could maintain the proper air of subtlety about this endeavor if we suddenly started a gunfight in the Galerie des machines, don't you agree?" Moran growled wordlessly and shook his head. "Do something with your friend there. Let's not alert the punters, shall we?" Fogg said. Moran frowned, but hefted the unconscious man, and set him down roughly on one of the benches that sat around the statue. "Good. Now, let's move to the front. If they can't take us unawares, they may be inclined to wait for a more opportune time."

"I say we take 'em now," Moran said, clenching and unclenching his fingers as they threaded through the crowd. "Throw the bastards off."

"To what end? We've spotted them. See—there, they're backing off," Fogg said, jerking his chin towards the assassins. They faded back into the crowd as the two men watched. "They don't want to alert the Sûreté, now do they? And nor do we." He glanced at Moran. "Unless you'd like to spend the remainder of our time here in a Parisian jail cell."

"They'd have to catch me first."

"Moriarty has policemen on his payroll, does he not? The war must have taught him that much—that it is best, when running an illicit enterprise, to have your people where you might need them," Fogg said.

"So?" Moran said.

"So what makes you think that this Enemy of yours has not come to the same conclusion? Why do you think Moriarty arranged for us to avoid contact with the authorities in Calais?" Fogg asked, as tranquilly as if he were discussing the weather. "Obviously, his arrangements were not entirely successful. Your Enemy is aware of us, and has sent men to trap us, a situation which we have obligingly walked into. And he almost certainly has men in place in the Sûreté and local constabulary, just waiting for us to make a mistake."

"Very clever, Fogg. But you're forgetting one thing," Moran said, after a moment.

"And what might that be?"

"He's your enemy as well," Moran said, grinning fiercely. He leaned close. "You're not clear of this, Eridanean." He caught hold of Fogg's lapel. "You'd do well to remember that our Enemy is your enemy, unless you want that heathen bride and those half-caste whelps of yours to wind up floating face-down in the Thames."

Fogg tensed, and a white-hot anger surged through him. Nonetheless, his face remained serene. "On the contrary, my good chap, I haven't forgotten at all," he said smoothly. "I am well aware of each and every one of my enemies." Moran's grin faded and he let go of Fogg's coat.

"Damn aliens; ice in your veins the lot of you," he muttered, looking away. If Moran had been hoping to provoke him, he obviously thought he'd failed. Fogg wondered why Moran felt the need to do so. Perhaps, he thought, he was merely a scapegoat for the frustration Moran likely felt in being put into their current situation by Moriarty. Fogg covertly examined Moran, and noted his increased respiration, pupil dilation, and inability to remain still. He gave silent thanks to the nameless pickpocket who'd filched Moran's pistol.

He turned his attention to the assassins who had spread out amongst the crowd. They were dressed to blend in, but as with the knife-man, they were not common ruffians, but something more subtle. He'd first noticed it on the ferry, but he was certain of it now. There was a predatory cant to their body language; Fogg guessed they were a society of some kind. They were trained in some lethal art or another, and had been trained together, or, at least by the same tutors. That spoke to a level of organization beyond which Fogg would expect from a common criminal conspiracy.

"They'll be on us as soon as this blasted crowd clears a bit," Moran said.

"Then we'd best move quickly. I'll go up the right set of stairs, you go left. Try not to make a scene," Fogg said. He fished his watch from his vest pocket and looked at it. "When were we to meet your contact?"

"Half twelve," Moran said.

"Twenty minutes, then. Would you care to describe them?"

"Not on your life," Moran said.

"Well then, you'd best see that you make the appointment," Fogg said. He snapped the watch shut and put it back into his vest pocket. Without waiting for Moran's reply, he made his way towards the stairs. He moved quickly, but without obvious hurry. Despite his assertions, he thought it quite likely the men following them didn't care about making a scene one way or another. Paris was no more a stranger to violence than London, and any untoward explosion of hostility would likely swiftly be relegated to a conflict between local gangs of pickpockets.

As he reached the top of the stairs, he saw one of the moving bridges dock. The stone beneath his feet trembled slightly as it did so. The moving bridges were railed platforms mounted on massive pneumatic arms that slid them across the open expanse between the upper galleries. The machinery that enabled them to move sat far below them, wheezing and grinding in a constant industrial rhythm. It reminded Fogg of the inner workings of a cotton gin or a manufacturing loom. Gears turned with a rattle and straps cycled loudly as the bridge settled and disgorged its occupants. Each bridge appeared able to hold at least thirty or forty people, and it took roughly twenty minutes to move across the gallery, according to Fogg's quick calculations.

He joined the next crowd as it filed onto the bridge. As it

ground into motion, he peered around, searching for Moran. There was no sign of him, however. Fogg had expected as much. He suspected Moriarty's operatives in Paris had clearly been co-opted or eliminated, given the number and proximity of enemy agents. That meant he and Moran had walked into the devil's trap, rather than catching the Enemy unawares; not that he had had much hope of that after the incident on the ferry and again on the train. Either Moriarty's grip on Paris was less certain than he'd thought, or Fogg had been misled. Both were equally possible. Fogg was beginning to get the feeling he was not so much a hunter as the bait. As he considered that bleak possibility, he reached for his watch, to check the time.

He felt the hand as it dipped into his pocket almost at the same time as his own, and grabbed the wrist it was attached to without turning around. Almost immediately, he was forced to let go of the would-be thief as a powerful punch nearly took him in the side. As it was, the blow grazed his hip, and sent him spinning around. He stumbled into another man, rebounded with an apology, and turned to face this new threat.

Fogg froze as the tip of the knife dug into his kidney. "Move and I'll spill your intestines here on the floor," a familiar voice murmured.

"I'm sure you would. The question is—why haven't you?" Fogg asked mildly. "Don't bother to answer. I'll save you the time. It's because your master wants me alive. Or at the very least, wants something I have." He stepped forward and turned. Gurn glared at him. The knife he held was a small, wide thing, like a tanner's scraping knife. He quickly slipped it into his coat as Fogg took a further step back. "He allowed Moran and I to get this close, after your ill-judged attempt to stymie us on the ferry." He spoke quickly.

"Ill-judged," Gurn murmured. His eyes were flat and opaque.

"Quite," Fogg said. "Where is he?" The crowd flowed around them, uncaring, attention occupied by the wonders around them and below them as the bridge trundled on towards its port of call on the other side of the gallery.

"You'll find out soon enough," Gurn said.

"Yes, I believe I will," Fogg said. He spun and delivered a stiff blow to the side of Gurn's head with his cane, felling the younger man instantly. Then, without hesitation, he grabbed onto the rail of the bridge and leapt up onto it, balancing perfectly. He tipped his hat to the suddenly attentive crowd and sprang across the gap between bridges.

People gasped and cried out as Fogg crashed into the rail of the other bridge and awkwardly hauled himself up and over. He looked back, but couldn't spot Gurn. He heard an uproar and turned to see several men pushing towards him through the crowd. Of course, he thought ruefully, they'd have men on all of the bridges, just in case.

The first shoved aside a squawking matron and came at him with a razor. Fogg whipped off his top hat and tossed it at his attacker, who caught it instinctively. Fogg's fist snapped forward and he caught the other man's jaw through the crown of the hat, pitching him backwards into the crowd, which set up an immediate cheer. He stripped the remains of his hat from his arm mournfully and let it fall to the ground below.

"Fogg! Look out," Moran bellowed, from somewhere in the milling crowd on the bridge opposite. He saw the burly colonel forcing his way through the crowd towards the side of his bridge, and following his gestures, Fogg saw an assassin taking a bead on him with a pistol. Instinctively, he ducked into the crowd, leaving a trail of apologies in his wake. He needed to get to the next bridge and Moran. He scrambled up onto the opposite rail. His shoes slipped beneath him, and rather than fall, he leapt again, reaching for the next moving bridge as it slowly grated past. He could hear a collective gasp from the crowd as he caught it, but just barely. The metal beneath him trembled as a bullet struck it. More shots followed, humming like wasps. The weapons were silenced somehow. Nonetheless, the human cargo crammed into the bridges knew something was up. Helping hands reached out to haul Fogg up.

"Quick thinking, Fogg," Moran said, "Couldn't have done it better myself."

"High praise," Fogg wheezed. "I—look out!" He shoved Moran back as a dark form hurtled across the gap, coat flapping like the wings of some great crow. Gurn landed on the rail with a heavy clang and made to propel himself off and onto Moran. Fogg reacted quickly. He jabbed his cane out like a spear and caught the young man in the belly.

Gurn wobbled, arms flailing comically as he lost his balance. His expression became perturbed as he slowly toppled backwards. The fall was a good sixty feet, and would, undoubtedly, prove fatal. Fogg leapt forward and caught the front of his shirt. "Grab my arm," he said. Gurn did so with alacrity. Fogg winced as the other man's fingers dug into his forearm. As he hauled the young man over the rail, he plucked the knife from the latter's coat. Before Gurn could protest, Fogg had the blade to his throat.

Gurn blinked. "You—saved me?" He said the words as if they were foreign to him.

"I did. I failed to save your friend on the train. I resolved not to let it happen a second time," Fogg said. "That said, I am not so naïve as to expect gratitude. So I shall hold this, and we shall get off the bridge together, you and I and the Colonel here."

"And then?" Gurn asked, still looking puzzled.

"And then, my friend, you will take me to where I need to go."

Eight

"I still don't understand why you saved the little bastard," Moran said as he wrenched Gurn's arm up behind his back and propelled him off the bridge and onto the upper gallery of the central dome to the applause of the crowd. A bit of quick blagging on Fogg's part had convinced those closest that he and Moran were agents of the Sûreté, and Gurn was an apache bound for the gaol. The young man gave no sign he felt any pain from Moran's rough treatment, save for a faint grimace.

"And that is why your master went to all of that trouble to recruit me," Fogg said, not looking at Moran. Instead, he examined Gurn. Then he reached for the young man's coat. He made a quick, but thorough search of their prisoner. "He doesn't have the distorter."

"Meaning what?"

"Meaning that we're close. Did Moriarty mention why his agents wanted to meet us here?" Fogg asked. He stroked his chin, considering. Moran hesitated. Fogg made a face. "Now is not the time to dither, Colonel. Did he?"

"No," Moran grated. He looked around, as if nervous.

"But the obvious should have occurred to you, yes?"

"Obvious ain't my field, Fogg," Moran said.

Fogg gestured with his cane at the gallery around them. "Look around you, Moran. Moriarty said he'd run the Enemy to ground. And he has. This, all around us, is his ground. You were right earlier—we are in the long grass, Moran. This is the Enemy's territory, and we are in it. Why else would he attack so openly? He could have struck at us in Calais, but he didn't—why? Because he was uncertain of the ground."

"The ferry . . ." Moran began.

"The ferry was a calculated risk. An attempt to deal with us quickly and in such a way as to throw off the suspicion of the authorities. Explosions on paddle-steamers are nothing new. Vessels sink in the Channel with depressing regularity. But when that failed, he waited, rather than striking again."

"What about the damn train? The balloon?" Moran demanded.

"You said it yourself, he divested us of your tools. It was their bad luck—and our good—that I interrupted them. He waited until we got to Paris, until we came to the Exposition, to make his move. Until we entered his side of the game board." As Fogg spoke, he watched Gurn's face. During his time as an agent, he'd made a study of what he'd come to call "sub-expressions"—the brief twitches of emotion that, when observed closely, could reveal a subject's true feelings. Gurn, while ostensibly stone-faced, displayed a wealth of such brief, almost invisible expressions.

"Gurn likely has orders to kill you. But me—for some reason, he wants me," Fogg said. From Gurn's face, he knew he was right. He didn't voice his suspicions as to why.

"That's obvious," Moran said, stroking his moustaches. He smiled unpleasantly. "You're bound for the torture rack, Fogg, or I'm a Chinaman's bride. Whatever questions he put to those others he caught, he wants to put to you as well. Hell, he's probably squeezed everything he can from your froggy servant." Moran chortled as he said it.

Fogg flinched inwardly at the thought, but didn't let it show on his face. Moran was trying to get a rise out of him, for whatever reason. Instead of responding, he looked at Gurn. "How did you get into the hall?" he said.

"What sort of question is that?" Moran asked.

"A pertinent one," Fogg said. "I'd guess that they have some subtle way in and out of here. How did you get in? More to the point, how did you intend to get me out?"

Gurn hesitated. Then he jerked his chin towards the curve of the dome. "The walls," he said.

Fogg nodded. "Of course," he said. He looked at Moran. "This structure, if I recall correctly, has no internal supports. The frame of the building is held up by trusses, as if it were a bridge. It's hollow, for the most part. Which means . . ." he trailed off.

"It's a hunter's blind," Moran said. He looked around. "They could be watching us right now."

"I have no doubt that they are. But if we are to do as your master wishes, and if we are to rescue my friend, then we have no choice but to cut our way into the blind, and confront the hunter face to face." Moran smiled.

"I like the way you think, Fogg." He grabbed Gurn. "Well? Lead the way, boy, or I'll wring your neck right here and now and God damn the consequences."

Gurn didn't protest. His docility immediately put Fogg on his guard. The likelihood of a trap was high. He led them along the upper gallery, through the crowd that moved across it. Fogg saw turbaned Arabs and Turks, and men in the uniforms of officers of a dozen armies from across the Continent. Women dressed in fashions from across Europe walked arm in arm with men dressed equally stylishly. The weird cadences of strange machines and foreign music drifted from further afield in the Exposition.

Gurn stopped in front of a panel set in the wall. He

looked around quickly, and tapped it in several place in sequence. There was a click, and the panel suddenly became loose in its frame. Moran grabbed him and thrust him back into Fogg's grasp. "Hold him," he said. Fogg took hold of Gurn, who offered up no complaint.

Moran led the way, his captured pistol in hand. Fogg followed, one hand on the back of Gurn's neck, and the other pressing his borrowed knife to his prisoner's side. The stairs were not unlike those found on metal gantries, and their footsteps echoed strangely as they entered the hidden alcove. The stairs led down to a series of platforms, each one slightly off-center from the one above it. The entire descent was lit by a series of oddly colored Crookes tubes which hung below the grating of each platform like strangely flickering fruits.

Moran pressed the barrel of his weapon to Gurn's head and muttered, "Where to now, you little blighter?"

Gurn smiled in a lopsided fashion and pointed his finger down. "Into the ninth circle," he said.

Moran looked at Fogg over their prisoner's shoulder. "Well Fogg? You're the brains here . . . what do you say?"

"I say the likelihood of this being a trap of some kind is high" Fogg said. "But as I said, I see no other option. If the Enemy is down there, then down there is where we must go."

Moran smirked. "A man after my own heart," he said. He turned and began to descend. Looking around as he followed, Fogg thought it fascinating the Enemy had somehow co-opted such an enormous national undertaking as the Exposition in order to build his lair. It implied a capacity for careful planning and misdirection as well as an uncommon patience that Fogg found disturbing in an opponent.

Moran paused. Fogg stopped Gurn from walking into him. "What is it?" he said.

"The air is circulating strangely down here all of a sudden," Moran said. He cocked his head. "Do you smell that? It was stale, before, but now it's growing fresher. It's like someone's opened a window, somewhere below."

"Or above us, perhaps," Fogg said. He leaned close to Gurn. "Is that it?"

Gurn's smile was a thing of unpleasant angles. Fogg drew back, as a sound filtered down from above—like the whisper of silk on metal. Gurn lunged forward, before Fogg could stop him, and, grabbing the rail, he vaulted over and dropped gracefully to the gantry below with a clang. Moran took a shot at him, but before they had a chance to see if he'd scored a hit, a lasso dropped down around his neck and suddenly pulled taut. Moran gagged and fired wildly up into the air. Fogg lashed out with his knife and cut the lasso, freeing Moran. But the respite was only momentary. More lassos dropped down out of the darkness above. They snagged Fogg's arms and throat. Moran was caught again. As the knots were pulled tight, Fogg's vision began to go dark. He saw dim shapes above him, circling as they hauled on the lassos and dragged him off his feet.

Then he saw nothing at all.

NINE

Fogg did not precisely awaken. He had not been unconscious, not truly. He'd been throttled to the point of passing out, but not over it. Even so, he was in no state to resist as he and Moran were lowered down and down and down even further still, into the darkness. Iron and steel were left behind, and replaced by hard, cold stone. Several times he drifted in and out of awareness, and by the time he'd recovered his faculties, both he and Moran were being shackled to a heavy pillar in a cavernous, low-ceilinged chamber.

There was a large organ, like the type often used in churches, occupying an alcove across from them. They had been shackled standing upright. There were more shackles, thankfully empty, dangling from the other, visible pillars. The chamber was dimly lit, by a series of old fashioned oil lanterns hanging from rusty hooks on several of the pillars. The chamber was filled with crates and boxes of various shapes and sizes.

Moran recovered quickly. He looked about with commendable calm. Fogg almost admired him in that moment. The Colonel displayed none of the panic or anxiety Fogg would have expected. As far as Moran was concerned, things might as well be going according to plan. Fogg lifted his head and looked around. The men who'd captured them stood at attention about them, as if waiting for something. Gurn sat on one of the heavy crates, Fogg's cane over his knees.

"So glad that you could join me, gentlemen," a voice said suddenly, echoing out of the shadows. "I have looked forward to this moment for some time. As, I suspect, have you." A cowled and robed figure moved through the shadows, a fine, if fraying cloak rustling in its wake. "You will have to forgive young Gurn his ferocity. I have tried to make a gentleman of him, but as you have seen, he is quite forceful. And my Vampires are little better. An offshoot of the Knights Hospitaller, if you can grasp such a thing. They found new ways and methods in the fertile soil of the Mediterranean, and became a league of shadows—thieves, murderers and spies-for-hire. I ran across them soon after my arrival in Paris, and judged them to be fractious neighbors, likely to cause complaint and difficulty. Thus, as with Gurn, I was forced to take them in hand—I hunted their Great Vampire across the rain-slick rooftops of the Rue d'Auseil one night and took his worthless life with a quick application of the my ever-faithful Punjab lasso." The cowled shape moved into the dim light, and swept lightly towards the organ. "They serve me now, and a better, more loyal crew one could hardly find. I trust that they did not harm you?"

"Not for lack of trying," Fogg said. It was impossible to tell whether the newcomer was a man or a woman, though he suspected the latter.

"I shall discipline them. Gurn, as I said, is somewhat headstrong. He never knew a mother's love or a father's steady hand, and it has broken him, I think. A more loveless creature I have never met—isn't that correct, my boy?"

Gurn looked up from playing with Fogg's cane. He cocked his head and examined the cowled figure, as the latter sat down at the organ. His face displayed no emotion, and his eyes were like two dollops of ink. He said nothing, but the cowled figure gave a breathy chuckle. "Do not be lulled, my friends. Though he wears his mask well, there is a roiling tempest beneath that bland gaze. He would be a beast, were it not for my tutelage. When I learned that he had taken it upon himself to blow up the ferry carrying you to me, I was quite incensed." The cowled figure tapped a few keys and sang softly for a few moments. His voice was startlingly lovely. "When I learned that you were coming, I saw no reason to hinder you. Gurn, however, is quite—ah—proactive in his outlook. He knows better, now."

From what Fogg could see, Gurn didn't look very repentant. Indeed, quite the opposite. Fogg recalled the expression on the young man's face as he'd confronted him on the ferry, and wondered if he were quite as beholden to his mysterious master as the latter seemed to think. He cleared his throat and said, "I'm sorry about the girl."

The cowled shape paused, then continued in its tinkering with the organ. "Ah, Irma, my little Irma. She will be missed, if she is indeed lost." He paused. "They are always missed, for a time."

"She fell from a train," Fogg said.

"And so she did," the cowled figure murmured. "Then, who hasn't?" The shape laughed. "She grew up on the rooftops of Paris, monsieur. She has had many a tumble, and will likely have more, if she continues on her chosen path. My Vampires regard her as something of a mascot. They were quite upset when she failed to return from her mission. The Vampires have always had little Irma to spur them on."

"The wolves are picking her bones by now," Moran said, rattling his chains. A Vampire struck Moran, punching him in the side. He groaned and cursed. The cowled shape waved a hand, and the Vampire stepped back.

"Baron Fogg, Phileas Fogg of Fogg Shaw, Derbyshire.

Formerly of No. 7 Savile Row, member in good standing of the Reform Club of Pall Mall and Piccadilly in London," the cowled shape sang artfully, plinking the keys of the organ for accompaniment. The cowl turned, revealing an ornately filigreed full-face mask, crafted after the fashion of those once worn by partygoers during the Renaissance. Strange, yellow eyes peered at Fogg and Moran from behind the mask. The lean, cloaked shape slid noiselessly to its feet after the gloved fingers played a final tune on the organ. "Colonel Sebastian Moran, late of India. Author of two seminal works on the sport of hunting. Good evening gentlemen, welcome to Paris," it—he rather, Fogg judged, from the timbre of the voice and the way he moved—said. He spoke English, with the barest trace of some indefinable accent. "I do hope that you have enjoyed your stay in Heaven's own city. It is a shame that you have come under such a cloud, and must depart so forcefully."

"Were we leaving then?" Fogg said. "I rather thought we had just arrived."

"Ah, English humor," their captor said. "But I am being rude. Forgive me. Men call me the Phantom. Welcome to my home."

"What sort of man lives in catacombs like these?" Fogg asked. But he already suspected that he knew the answer. He'd heard of the Phantom of the Paris Opera House, and the deaths that he'd caused. If this were the same man, then he and Moran were in a more perilous situation than he'd feared.

"No man at all, some might say," the Phantom said. "I have been called both a monster and an angel." He pressed his hands to his chest, as if preening before an audience. "But, until recently, I have been the Opera Ghost, the Phantom of the *Palais Garnier*." He waited, like a showman expecting applause.

PHILEAS FOGG AND THE WAR OF SHADOWS

Fogg frowned. "That name strikes me as familiar. When I was last in Paris some eight years ago, I recall some scandal about an opera singer."

"Ah, yes, then you have indeed heard of me," the Phantom said, sweeping out his hands and bowing low. "But speak no more of those days. It is in the past, and we are on the cusp of the future." He hesitated. "Though, might I inquire as to how you came to learn of such a sad incident?"

"An individual of my acquaintance mentioned it to me, in connection to a box in the Palais Garnier I had wished to rent," Fogg said, slowly. "He called you a devil."

"Ah, as I suspected and so I am—and was this individual of an oriental persuasion, perhaps? A man who served as *daroga* at the pleasure of the Shah of Persia, in the rosy hours of Mazenderan?" the Phantom asked.

"He vanished, not long after we'd left Paris," Fogg said. The Persian, a man named Nadir, had been an Eridanean agent, first in Persia, and then, later, in Paris. From his tiny flat in the Rue de Rivoli, Nadir and his servant Darius had been employed in much the same manner as Fogg himself, foiling Capellean plots in France and the rest of Europe. The Persian had been relieved when he learned of the war's end—he was far too noble and generous of heart to be an effective agent, in Fogg's estimation. "I assumed that he'd gone home."

"Sadly, he did not," The Phantom said. He clasped his hands in front of him. "He was a good friend to me, in those early years. But as with all childish things, friendship must eventually be put aside for the greater good." He strode towards them. "You see, even as he kept my secret, I learned of his. That he, that most humane of men, was not human at all. Less even than I," he said.

Fogg said nothing. The peculiar yellow eyes examined him the way he fancied a child might look at a butterfly, just before they plucked its wings. He returned his captor's gaze, taking the opportunity to study the Phantom up close. What was this creature, he wondered—the Phantom was not an Eridanean, or Capellean, nor was he wholly a man, not with those yellow eyes and that abnormally thin frame. Moran snorted. "Hard to believe that, frankly."

The Phantom whirled, his cloak flaring and snapping as he turned his gaze on Moran. "And what would you know of it?" He leaned towards Moran and tugged playfully on his moustache. "You are nothing special—a gunman. Pfaugh! I can have twenty men as good as you, simply by scouring the deserts of North Africa. Gurn is twice the killer you are, and less than half your age," he said, gesturing to the young man, where he sat watching the exchange. Gurn sneered slightly, as Moran's face turned beet-red and then purple with rage.

"I know more than you think, you urine-eyed sneak-thief," Moran snarled. His chains clattered as he thrust himself vainly towards the Phantom, who hastily backed away. "They call you the Phantom, but I know what you are—a carnival freak. You belong in a bloody cage, like the wild man from Borneo and the rest of God's mistakes!"

The Phantom tensed. Fogg saw the blow coming before the man's arm moved, but even so, he was impressed with the speed of that frail-seeming limb. Moran's head snapped back from the blow. He shook himself, like a stunned bullock. Moran spat blood and bared his teeth like one of the tigers he'd become famous for bagging. Then, without further pause, he unleashed a torrent of verbal abuse on his captor. The Phantom turned away. He gestured to Gurn, and the other guards. "Take him to the oubliette. Let him curse the darkness, if he so wishes."

Moran continued to spew obscenities. He thrashed in his bonds, eyes blazing. The Phantom gestured again, airily. His men unhooked Moran from the wall, and dragged him bodily from the chamber. Moran kicked and cursed in what Fogg thought to be a most undignified fashion the entire way. The Phantom watched him go, and then turned back to Fogg with a shrug. "Some men, they can't help but pollute the air, eh?"

"He was quite charming on the Channel crossing," Fogg said.

"Really?"

"No." Fogg looked at him. "Where are they taking him?"

"Paris, much like your beloved London, is built upon the bones of older cities. The infamous catacombs are but the barest tip of what lurks beneath the City of Lights, Monsieur Fogg. There are appropriate holes where a crass beast like the good Colonel may be stashed. But for now, let us discuss other, less pleasant things."

"Less pleasant than Moran?"

The Phantom laughed. "Quite. Hard to credit, I know." He snapped his fingers. "Gurn, my boy. Unlock our guest's manacles. I would have his opinion on certain matters which have occupied my mind of late."

TEN

"Now, monsieur, a test," the Phantom said, once Fogg had been freed. "Tell me, where do you think you are, at this moment?" Fogg rubbed his aching wrists and looked about. If the Phantom wanted to play guessing games, who was he to say no? It would give him more time to formulate a plan of escape, at any rate. He examined the stone and the dirt; he sniffed the air and tapped the iron trusses which supported the ceiling. He considered to whom he was speaking.

"Simple. We are beneath the Eiffel Tower, which has only recently opened to the public," Fogg said calmly. "I'd warrant, given what little I have heard of you, that you had some small input into its construction and design, even as you supposedly did for the Palais Garnier."

"Ha! Magnificent, monsieur! Simply wonderful," the Phantom crowed. "Your reputation for ratiocination is not undeserved, I see." He swept his cloak about him and strode to one of the columns. "It has been too long since I could properly share the secrets of my artifice with an appreciative audience. Gurn listens, but—ah!—he does not appreciate!" With a single motion, he opened a hidden cabinet built into the stone pillar, to reveal a convex curve of glass. Fogg, astonished, saw the glass showed what he guessed were the upper levels of the Eiffel Tower. The Phantom grabbed the handle of an iron crank mounted below the glass and began to turn it. As he did so, the scene on the glass slowly rotated. The Phantom continued to turn the crank until the glass showed the city of Paris, in all of its glory. The sun was setting, and the City of Lights was living up to its name.

"I did indeed have some small input into the creation of the edifice beneath which we shelter. Thousands of carefully shaped, silvered, and angled mirrors line its frame, hidden from sight, but enabling me to see everything." He turned and gestured to the other columns. "Each of these pillars hides a similar spying glass. Some are even strewn throughout the Exposition—oh, the things I have seen, monsieur. Did you know that the American sharpshooter, Annie Oakley, sings the most delightful, if rough-hewn, ballads to herself when she is alone in her quarters here? I have listened on many occasions, and I fancy that I could do wonders with that voice, were she so inclined. I have seen Sybil Sanderson sing the lead in that hack Massenet's *Esclarmonde*, and hung in the shadowed trusses above the Javanese ensemble as they made the most extraordinary music. Yes, with these mirrors, I can keep watch on my city from the safety and solitude of this stone womb. Like God in his Heaven, or the Devil in his Hell, I conduct my war from beneath the Field of Mars."

"War," Fogg repeated.

"War," the Phantom said. "I, whom the hand of all mankind is turned against, have discovered a threat that no man can defeat. A cloying, cunning conspiracy of alien intelligences, whose machinations have shaken the foundations of history. A conspiracy which, until recently, you were a part of, were you not?"

Fogg hesitated. Then, "Yes."

The Phantom seemed to deflate for a moment. Then he

nodded. "Then I am not mad. I feared I was, even as I pursued the only course which seemed open to me."

"By which you mean the kidnap and murder of innocent men and women. Including my manservant, Jean Passepartout," Fogg said sharply.

"Innocent—innocent? They were as guilty as any anarchist or Bolshevik. As guilty as you." The Phantom paused. "I do not know the name you have mentioned, however. I have taken no one in weeks, since my failure to acquire a professor of mathematics in your fair country. And him—well, he's no innocent, that is a certainty. Not when he employs creatures like your companion, the Colonel."

"Moriarty," Fogg said. For some reason, he believed his captor. There was a persuasive rhythm to the Phantom's words, like the hypnotic purr of a cat. That meant Passepartout had escaped. He felt a surge of relief, and a renewed sense of determination. He had to escape. Fogg shook his head. "You tried to capture Moriarty."

"Why would I not, when he has made himself such an obstacle to my activities? At first, I thought him merely a rival of the Vampires, but then, in my inquisition, I learned his true identity. So, I prepared myself for war."

"But that's not the only reason you're here, is it?" Fogg said.

The Phantom inclined his head. "No, it is not."

Fogg licked his lips. "What else did you do to the Tower?" he said.

The Phantom paused. "What do you think I did?" he asked, preening slightly.

"When you showed me the upper sections of it just now, I saw something familiar," Fogg said slowly. The Phantom chuckled.

"I should hope so," he said. He turned the crank again, returning to the previous view. Fogg stared at the image and blinked slowly, the only outward sign of the sudden wave of consternation he felt. There was no doubt about it—the design of the Eiffel Tower mimicked the internal mechanisms of a distorter!

It was brilliant, in its way. The singular flaw in all attempts of which Fogg was aware to recreate the distorters using current technologies was that it was all but impossible to replicate the internal mechanisms at the proper size. But the Phantom had simply bypassed that issue by increasing the scale of the internal clockwork a thousand times over.

"You see it, of course," the Phantom said. "It is an imperfect design, much like myself, but powerful for all that. Beneath these catacombs are the great water-engines which power my creation. I draw upon the strength of the Seine, the very life's blood of Paris, to send my Vampires fluttering across the country to wreak my will."

"But two distorters are required for transport," Fogg said. He'd seen the bulky watch in Gurn's possession. A picture was beginning to form in his mind, and it wasn't at all a pleasant one.

"Ah, and that is where human ingenuity comes in, my alien friend," the Phantom said. "The distorters are not separate devices, as you and your kind claimed—no! Instead, they are two halves of the same device, much like the electric telephone devised by the American, Bell. A transmitter and a receiver are, independent of one another, useless, but together they are a powerful tool."

"Nonetheless, you still require two," Fogg said.

"True, but they do not require equal components," the Phantom said. Fogg detected a faint air of smugness about the Phantom's words. He was about to respond, when the import of the Phantom's words dawned on him. He sank back against the pillar.

"Of course," he said. The distorters were designed to act as both receivers and transmitters; as long as you possessed both, or were within range of one, you could travel. Beyond size, that was another obstacle to the production of new devices. "The tower is your transmitter."

"I knew you were canny, monsieur. Yes, Eiffel's grand edifice is a transmitter. Thanks to its size, and the materials used in its construction, it has a massive range. Nonetheless, it has its limits." The Phantom drew himself up. "Come," he said, and swept out of the chamber after plucking an oil lamp from a stanchion on the wall. Fogg hurried after him, Gurn trotting in his wake. He could feel the latter's eyes boring into his back.

Fogg didn't bother to ask where they were going. Instead, he examined the walls and floor, and took note of all the twists and turns they took, memorizing them. Given what he knew of Paris, and the grounds above, he was beginning to form a mental picture of the catacombs. If he got the chance, it might help him to escape. He glanced over his shoulder at Gurn, who smiled thinly. Fogg turned back. Unfortunately, such a chance was beginning to look like the remotest of possibilities.

The corridor they were in began to slope downwards, and Fogg could feel the chill of some unseen tributary of the Seine emanating from the damp stones. The walls spread, and the corridor flowered into a circular grotto of stone archways, each one opening up onto a small chamber. The light from the Phantom's lamp passed over these, casting strange shadows on the dark stones that comprised them. For a moment, Fogg thought he was back in the strange chamber in the Fogg Shaw Barrow. He pushed the thought aside. There were similarities, but that was as far as it went.

A single iron pylon occupied the center of the chamber, like the spoke of a wheel. It speared through the floor and ceiling both, and Fogg knew without being told it was connected to the great structure that crouched far above them. He looked around. "This is where you send them out."

"And bring them back," the Phantom said. He gazed about himself admiringly. "I thought it appropriate."

Fogg paused before an archway. A distressingly familiar odor hung heavy on the wet air. He touched the slick stones. "Roman," he said.

"*Lutetia Parisorum*," the Phantom intoned. "These are its bones." The smell grew stronger, and Fogg made to step away from the arch, when suddenly, the Phantom was behind him. "This was once part of an amphitheatre. It was a waiting area for gladiators, before they went to shed blood on the sands somewhere above. Now, it shelters a different sort of warrior."

The Phantom held the lamp aloft and the soft, flickering light revealed a scene of grotesque horror on the other side of the arch. Fogg fought back a sudden wave of nausea as he gazed at the twisted, ruined things which lay on the stone floor. No, he realized, with mounting horror, not on, so much as *in*. The bodies of the Vampires were contorted and stretched in grisly fashion, and their limbs and bodies were half-sunken into the stone floor and stretched across the back wall of the catacomb in a nightmarish fashion. Their flesh had warped and liquefied, congealing in an abominable manner. Fogg fancied they had been exposed to an intense heat and then an equally intense cold. He could make out three semi-distinct faces amidst the monstrosity before him, and hoped, for their sake, that they had died instantly.

"A molecular crash," Fogg murmured. He'd heard rumors of such occurring, when something went wrong with a distorter. Rather than appearing hale and whole, the traveler's molecular structure was jammed into the largest source of matter nearby. The Vampires had become part of the catacombs. There was no way of telling where the men ended and the stones began.

The Phantom nodded. "There is a term for it then. Good," he said. "If someone has a word for it, then means that there is possibly a way to see that it doesn't happen again."

"These are the men who attacked the *Calais/Douvres*," Fogg said, looking at his captor.

"They were, yes. Not all of them," the Phantom said. "Gurn, as you have seen, survived, albeit quite wet." He gestured back towards Gurn with the lamp. The latter was staring at Fogg with a steady, chilling gaze. The young man's face was almost terrifying in the weak light, though Fogg would have been hard pressed to say why. There was something of the devil in Gurn. Of the three of them, Gurn was at once the most and least human; The Phantom was an outcast by dint of his appearance, and Fogg had been raised by aliens. What was Gurn's excuse?

"Your attempt to reverse engineer the distorters was flawed," Fogg said.

"Obviously so," the Phantom said. Gurn stepped towards the hecatomb and peered at the blistered and twisted contents. He smiled faintly, and Fogg repressed a shudder. He was fighting to keep his mind calm. The stress of the situation had threatened to overwhelm him more than once since he'd been brought below. He felt the Phantom's yellow eyes on him. "You see now, why I wanted to meet you."

"No," Fogg said.

"Is that a question or an answer?"

"Both," Fogg said, "Neither." He met the Phantom's gaze steadily. "The distorters are gone. Even I do not know where they are. Your efforts to capture me have been for nothing."

"Efforts?" the Phantom asked. He cocked his head. "I have made no effort to capture you, Monsieur Fogg. Indeed, I thought you too cunning for such a scheme. Little did I know that you would wander into my grasp. The gods surely smile upon their most unfortunate child." He looked at Gurn. "Take him. It is time to put him to the question."

Eleven

"But why?" Fogg said, as he was shackled to the pillar once more by Gurn. "Why all of this?" The Phantom had ordered him brought back to the central chamber. As Fogg was restrained, the Phantom busied himself with a brazier that had been brought into the chamber in their absence. A rack of age-blackened iron tools sat near it, and periodically, the Phantom would select one and set it into the simmering coals in the brazier. Fogg recalled the descriptions of the bodies Moriarty had given him, and knew the same fate awaited him. "Why the distorters, why the kidnappings—why?"

"Why?" the Phantom said, as if in disbelief. "Would you ask the Greek partisan why he resisted the invading Turk?" He swept close to Fogg, his yellow eyes blazing. "You have invaded my world. And I intend to throw you back into whatever cosmic void you and your kind crawled out of. I am the hero of this performance, sirrah. I am Don Juan, and I will be triumphant."

Fogg shook his head. "The war is over, the conspiracy you fight against is done."

"Is it? For you perhaps," the Phantom said, turning away.

"Don't you understand? The men and women you've

tortured and killed were no more alien than you. The last pure member of either race has long since perished."

"And what of the other races, eh? What of those other invisible empires which wrangled with your own?"

Fogg felt his mouth go dry. He recalled his own speculations in that regard, and wondered what his captor had discovered. He needed to know. "What other races?" he asked.

The Phantom looked at him, eyes narrowed behind his mask. "Don't play the fool. I have been told about you. I know that you were more than a mere captain in that war you claim is over. You must know. After all, why else would you make your redoubt where you have?"

"My . . ." Fogg's voice trailed off as the Phantom's words sunk in. "The barrow," he said softly. "What do you know about it?"

"Nothing which is of any import to you, in your current circumstances. Gurn, go check on our other guest," the Phantom said. Gurn left the chamber reluctantly. Fogg fought to control the panic he felt rising in his gut. The Phantom turned back to him. "Now, before I put you to the question, I have one, final request. Your watch," he said, gesturing flamboyantly. Like a true showman, he'd waited for the perfect moment to make the demand of his captive audience.

"In my vest," Fogg said slowly. He pushed aside all thought of the barrow or the implications of what the Phantom had just told him. He needed to concentrate on survival and escape. The Phantom took his watch and, with a powerful tug, tore the cloth and snapped the chain. He stepped back to examine it, murmuring to himself. Fogg's thoughts crystallized and he knew, without any further doubts, why so much attention had been paid to his choice of timepiece. "That is what Irma was looking for when I encountered her on the train, I presume," he said carefully. "And why you were upset with Gurn for his attempt to kill us."

Phileas Fogg and the War of Shadows

The Phantom ignored Fogg, and continued to inspect the watch. Fogg went on, "I was puzzled, at first. But it became readily apparent what your motivation was, especially after you boasted about your technological feats. Somehow, you gained a set of schematics and built a working, if flawed, distorter. But those flaws render it almost useless. You didn't truly want me. You wanted my distorters."

The Phantom suddenly hurled the watch aside. It smashed against a pillar and shattered. The Phantom lunged for Fogg, like a falcon sighting its prey, and began to tear at his clothes. "Where is it? Where is it?" he hissed, eyes blazing with a sickly light. He tore the lining from Fogg's pockets, and pawed at his clothes. "You must have another somewhere. I was told that you—"

"That I what? Carried a distorter on my watch-fob?" Fogg said. "And who told you that, I wonder?" The Phantom stopped in his frantic search. His strange eyes found Fogg's own. He blinked, slowly, as comprehension dawned. Then, his composure restored as suddenly as it had vanished, the Phantom stepped back. Fogg pressed on. "We've both been tricked, I'm afraid. I suspected as much, but I couldn't be sure. Nemo—Moriarty—has been feeding you disinformation for some time, I expect. It was a common enough gambit of his, in the war between our peoples. He was adept at wielding information like a blade, giving you just enough to cut yourself."

"So you say, but why?" The Phantom murmured.

Before Fogg could reply, the room shook with a dull roar. The Phantom stumbled, but swiftly regained his balance and spun, reaching for one of the speaking tubes attached to the wall. He shouted into it, demanding a report. If he'd asked, Fogg could have told him what he needed to know. Moran was loose, and the Phantom's defenses had been breached.

It was all so clear now, at the sharp end of things.

Moriarty, like Fogg himself, had a mind like an onion. Every thought, every scheme, every ploy, hid another. Plots within plots. Fogg was tainted meat, fed to the tiger, and Moran the shikari. Moriarty had told him as much, but he hadn't grasped the full measure of the thing until too late. Moriarty had been right—retirement had dulled Fogg's edge and made him complacent.

He had been used to draw the Phantom out. Now Moran, true to his nature, was making his kill. The Phantom stood frozen for a moment, and Fogg wondered if he suffered from the same malady as Moriarty. Then, he realized that rather than the paralysis of indecision, what he was witnessing was the stillness of a predator judging where best to leap. The Phantom sprang into motion a moment later. He ripped one of the cavalry sabres down from the wall and flourished it with aplomb. "Moriarty has loosed a tiger in my donjon, it seems. Ah, but I have hunted tigers before. I shall run the beast to ground and have its pelt for my wall, eh, monsieur? And then, after, we shall speak of distorters and watch-fobs, yes?"

Without waiting for a reply, the Phantom bounded for a wall and pressed his palm to a particular stone. There was a grinding noise, and the squeal of unseen gears, and a section of the wall slid aside, revealing a hidden aperture. Wrapping his cloak about him, the Phantom stepped into the darkness and vanished. As he disappeared, the stone aperture began to close. Fogg waited until it had sealed itself. Then he began plucking at a loose thread in his coat sleeve.

He had expected some form of treachery, but never so soon, and never in the enemy's lair. To summarily sacrifice half of your forces before the battle was done smacked of lunacy. Then, Moran was the sort of man for whom innumerable enemies merely meant a wealth of targets. The thread came away easily in his grasping fingers, and revealed the rounded grip of a lockpick. His fingers ached with the strain of it, but he was able to get a grip on the tool and slowly, carefully, he began to extract it from its hidden pocket.

The chamber shuddered as another explosion rocked the catacombs. Moran seemed intent on tearing the place apart stone by stone. Fogg wondered how he was managing it. A cache of gunpowder was the obvious culprit, but these catacombs didn't seem conducive to keeping such a compound dry and useable. Moran had likely brought something in with him. The chamber shuddered again, and a loose stone fell down, bouncing off the organ and striking the floor. The dust of centuries sifted down, and Fogg's heart rate elevated. He fought to keep calm, to reroute the panicky impulses trying to gain purchase in his mind to somewhere less bothersome, but it was difficult. Several times, his sweat slick fingers lost their grip on the lockpick. Once he thought he'd dropped it.

He wondered what would happen, if he should perish here? Would Aouda and his daughters be safe? Or would Moriarty hunt them down, simply to finish the job? And what of Passepartout? What had happened to him? And besides these worries, he had other, more disquieting considerations now, thanks to the Phantom.

These thoughts spurred him on. Fogg redoubled his efforts to extract the lockpick. He could smell smoke now, creeping down the passageways. The catacombs might as well be a massive chimney flue. All of the ways that fresh air was circulated through the tunnels would just as easily draw the smoke. The place would be a tomb within the hour. But that wouldn't satisfy Moriarty—no, there was another goal here. He and the Phantom were the birds and Moran the stone, but what was the goal? Not simply the eradication of a threat, for Moriarty could simply have assaulted the Phantom's lair if he'd wished.

The distorters. That was it! Fogg stifled a curse. Of

course—it all made sense. Moriarty had been obsessed with devising his own distorters during the war. He had ultimately failed, but Fogg doubted he had given up. If he'd learned the Phantom was close to developing a working distorter, Moriarty would have been desperate to acquire it. It was just his bad luck the Phantom had chosen the Eiffel Tower as the transmitter. But it wouldn't be a total loss. Not if he scavenged what he could from the Phantom's workshop, which was likely located in the catacombs somewhere. But first, the enemy had to be driven out.

He heard the sound of running feet, and froze, wondering if the Phantom was returning. Had Moran been run to ground so quickly then?

His question was answered a moment later as a burly figure, stinking of chemicals and smoke, burst into the chamber, weapon ready. "Back so soon?" Fogg asked, as calmly as he was able. "Accommodations not to your liking then, Colonel?"

Moran looked as if he'd been caught in a house-fire. He grinned through a mask of soot. "Not quite. Not a fan of these froggy hotels. Terrible service," he said. "Glad to see you're still where I left you, though. I was afraid that you'd run off."

"Perish the thought," Fogg said. "The recent cacophony was your doing then?"

"Himself has a way with explosives. Two separate compounds, that when mixed can tear open a blockhouse." Moran gestured towards his feet. "One in each hollow bootheel. They never check your footwear, these Continentals. The strength of the English detective is in his innate suspicion of everything." He stuffed his pistol through his belt and moved to the door. "Half a tick, just need to see about that draft," he said.

Fogg carefully inserted the lockpick he'd extracted into

the ancient lock of the manacles. The shackles were close to a century old, and of a type he was familiar with. He suspected it would be best to free himself as quickly as possible. He doubted Moran had come to rescue him.

"That was Moriarty's plan, then? To get you into the Phantom's lair so that you could destroy his experimental distorter?" Fogg said hurriedly, trying to distract Moran. The other man chuckled hoarsely as he closed the chamber door and barred it. When he turned back around, he had plucked the pistol from his belt once more.

Moran hefted the weapon. "Galand," he said. He spun the smooth cylinder, listening to it click. "Double action, 1870. Fiddly bit of kit, like most froggy guns. Still, it'll do the job until I find the little sneak who took my Mauser." He looked at Fogg, and smiled. "And of course it was. What did you think I was coming out here for? He was too smart to pop up out in the open, our ghostly friend, so an airgun was out. That left crawling down the drain, after the tiger. But before you do that, you need to damn well make sure the tiger's home," Moran said. "Cheers for that, by the by."

"It must have frightened Moriarty, to think that a lunatic like the Phantom had a working distorter," Fogg said, ignoring the jibe.

Moran laughed. "Made his eyes start out of his head like you wouldn't believe," he said. "But when he started to think about it, well . . . then he saw the opportunity. He saw a chance to whack two stoats with one brick, as it were." He shook his head. "Oh, he's a funny fellow, Himself. Got a nasty sense of humor," he said. He cocked the revolver, and grimaced. "Listen to that cocking mechanism. If I hadn't bashed in his skull already, I'd be tempted to give its former owner a thumping," he grunted.

"I assumed I was to be a sacrificial lamb, rather than a tethered kid," Fogg said as his fingers worked quickly on the locks to his cuffs. If he didn't get them open, he was as good as dead. That Moran intended to kill him was plainly obvious. He looked around the chamber, and sighted his sword cane sitting where Gurn had left it.

"Not much difference, to my way of thinking," Moran said, taking aim. "If it helps, Himself never had your woman or your brats. She was too slippery for us. And your man-servant as well." Moran sighted down the barrel of the pistol. "We'll get them, though. Himself doesn't forgive or forget. They'll all die, one by one, and join you in Hell before you have a chance to get lonely."

As Moran spoke, Fogg felt rather than heard the manacles click open. Before the other man could react, Fogg jerked his arms down and dropped to the floor. The pistol roared but Fogg was already moving. He darted around behind the column. Moran cursed, and made to follow. Fogg was careful to keep the column between them. Smoke was filling the chamber, drifting through the carven flues that kept the air cycling through the catacombs. The door Moran had closed and barred rattled in its frame as something heavy struck it.

Moran whirled as the wooden bar cracked. Fogg lunged for him, grabbing for his gun hand. Moran's elbow caught him in the gut, and Fogg staggered back. Moran spun back around and Fogg found himself staring down the barrel of the revolver. "Time to die, Fogg," Moran said.

The door burst open, and a gout of smoke whooshed into the chamber. Moran turned and Fogg ducked away, scrambling across the floor towards the last place he'd seen his sword cane. Given the situation, he'd have preferred a pistol, but any weapon was better than none at this point. He heard Moran yelling obscenities as he fired, and a reply from the men who'd stormed the chamber. Fogg snatched up his cane and rolled towards the organ, hoping its bulk might protect him from any stray shots until he worked out his next move.

The chamber was filled with smoke now, and Fogg's lungs were burning with the weight of it. Shots still cascaded through the room, piercing the building gloom with bursts of flame and noise. He wondered if the participants could even see who they were shooting at.

He needed to get out, and let whatever was happening, happen without him. Through the smoke, he noticed he was near the wall the Phantom had vanished through earlier. It might be an exit. At the very least, having a wall of stone between him and a stray bullet was better than the current state of affairs.

He moved to it, and touching the same stone as the Phantom had, opened the hidden door. As gunshots and explosions rocked the chamber behind him, Fogg plunged into the darkness.

Twelve

The corridor was dark, as the aperture resealed itself behind him. Fogg placed his free hand on the wall to guide his path. He had discarded his sword cane's sheath, and carried the naked blade extended slightly before him. The sound of gunshots and explosions faded, as he walked. He passed several apertures he took to be hidden doors much like the one through which he'd entered. Soon, the only sound he could hear was his own breath rasping in his lungs. The darkness closed in around him as tightly as a giant's fist. Water splashed at his ankles as he walked, and he wondered if the Phantom were flooding his lair.

The answer to that question came quickly enough, when he saw a pale square of darkness floating before him on the floor. As he drew closer, he saw it was a shaft of light, and that the fresh air was coming with it, as well as water by the bucketful. He stepped into the light and was rewarded by a heavy spatter of rain on his upturned face. There were iron rungs attached to the wall. He climbed them quickly, despite the fact they were slick with rain, and found himself once more beneath the Eiffel Tower, which loomed above him. Rainwater sluiced down its iron frame, and splashed loudly across the stones. The thunderstorm had only grown in strength, since they'd entered the Phantom's lair.

He heard a cackle of laughter, and saw a shadowy shape scramble up the stairs onto the tower. The Phantom had obviously realized Moran had doubled back on him. If Fogg had been in his shoes, he'd have sought the quickest means of egress. Even as he pursued, he wondered where the Phantom was going. Surely there was no way to escape up there, if escape was what he intended. Unless, of course, the madman intended to use a balloon or his flawed distorter. Fogg wouldn't have put either past the lunatic, but he knew he couldn't let the Phantom escape. He had his own questions to put to his adversary.

The lights of Paris spun beneath him as he climbed the stairs towards the top of the Eiffel Tower, his sword cane gripped tightly in his hand. He could just make out the flapping, batlike shape of the Phantom's cloak above him, moving through the shadowed reaches of the structure. The Phantom, frustrated performer to the last, was waiting for him somewhere above. This was confirmed a moment later, when the Phantom's crawling laughter slithered down to lash him. "Come, come, monsieur! Attend me, here in the heights!" the Phantom cried out. Fogg climbed on, grimly. "Climb, alien! Climb!" the Phantom urged and cackled.

Fogg climbed on, until he was winded, and soaked to the bone by the wind-blown rain. As he reached the observation deck, he caught sight of the Phantom. The mask reflected the lights of the city as it glared at him from the shadows. Fogg, determined to give his opponent no chance to attack, made a stamping lunge. The tip of his blade struck metal and the mask fell to the ground. Fogg became conscious of his mistake only a moment before the Phantom launched his attack.

His saber slashed out, nearly taking Fogg's head. He stepped out of the darkness where he'd been crouched, and

Fogg froze as he caught sight of his opponent's unmasked features. It was like looking into the face of a corpse, almost fleshless and leering. Thin strands of black hair were plastered to the yellow scalp by the rain, and the lipless mouth grinned murderously as its owner slid forward and sank into a duelist's stance.

There was a murderous elegance to the man, Fogg thought, as he retreated quickly, parrying a second blow with his blade. And he was strong, as well. Fogg's cane shivered in his grip as he parried a second blow and launched his own. The fight continued in that vein for several moments, the only sounds the clash of blades, the soft growl of the wind, and the squeak of their shoes on the metal floor of the deck.

"They say my father was a beast, you know," the Phantom said, as they broke apart and circled one another. "A devil in the flesh, and that is why I am as you see me. If that is true, he gave me more than this abominable countenance," he continued, gesturing to his repellent features. "I do not grow old, Fogg. And I am ungodly strong. I am a titan among men. My mind, my cunning, my frame, all of it superior. But I am forced to squat in catacombs and curtained opera boxes because of this damned flesh. If there is a God, I am his most vicious joke. And I am tired of it!" He stamped forward, his blade arcing in an overhand slash. Fogg barely turned aside the blow, such was the speed and strength of it.

"I tire of being a ghost," the Phantom went on. "I would be a hero. And you will help me. I will strip your secrets from you. I will scour the world, and find all that you have hidden. I will make you sing for me, Fogg. I will make you reveal everything!"

Fogg found himself being steadily forced backwards, until his spine connected with the railing. He had no breath to spare for a rejoinder. The Phantom was faster and stronger than he'd anticipated. He came at Fogg in a rush, cloak flaring out around him like an all-consuming shadow. Their blades locked. The Phantom's cadaverous face leered at him, over the crossed blades. He pushed close to Fogg. "Look behind you, monsieur, look! If Paris is heaven, then I am the devil," he hissed. "And the devil defends his own."

Over the Phantom's shoulder, Fogg saw a shape moving up onto the deck. Something gleamed in the moonlight. He heard the *click* of a pistol being cocked. The Phantom did as well. His eyes widened, and he shoved Fogg back, nearly over the rail, and whirled, blade flashing out. There was a gunshot and a cry. Then, as he steadied himself, Fogg saw the Phantom clutch his arm and stagger back, his blade stained crimson. He'd been shot, but nowhere vital, more was the pity, and he'd managed to stab his attacker, Fogg saw.

Gurn clutched his chest, where the Phantom's blade had caught him, and he lay slumped against the opposite rail. Fogg could only guess what had prompted the young killer to pursue them up into the dark. As he watched, Gurn reached up, grabbed the rail and hauled himself to his feet. Blood stained his arm and chest. He was obviously in pain, but as ever, his face displayed nothing.

"Judas!" the Phantom hissed.

"No," Gurn said. "But I pay my debts." His dark gaze met Fogg's own, but briefly, before flicking to his pistol, laying nearby. The Phantom took his sword in his good hand and extended it.

"Don't," he said. "I saved you, boy. I can dispose of you, just as easily."

Gurn lunged for the pistol. The Phantom slid forward, his eyes blazing. Fogg heard the sound of steel piercing flesh and then Gurn toppled forward, soundlessly. The Phantom whipped around, his ghastly face contorted into a rictus of hatred. "He was the best of them, the little fool. He would have been my heir, in time. Now he is simply another broken device, like my great distorter." He pointed his bloody blade at Fogg. "You owe me a debt of blood, Englishman. And I intend to collect every drop over the coming days and weeks."

Fogg tensed. Every muscle ached, and he was riding on the ragged edge of complete physical and mental collapse. The strain and tension of the whole affair was building within him, eating away at him from within. He felt as if he were a boiler being run past the point of safety. If he was to have any hope of surviving the next few moments, he would have to force his opponent to make a misstep.

He brought his blade up in a casual salute. "If you would have it, Monsieur Gargoyle, come and take it," he said, with every ounce of supercilious calm he could muster. He saw the Phantom's eyes widen in rage. After everything that had happened, the Phantom's almost superhuman calm had become frayed at the edges. With a shriek, his opponent hurled himself forward. He smashed aside Fogg's defenses, battering him backwards, his strength only seeming to grow, despite his wound. As Fogg's back struck the rail again, he reached out with his free hand and grabbed hold of the rain-slick metal. He kicked out, driving his opponent back. The Phantom came at him again in a wild rush, all traces of grace and poise lost in his monstrous *berserkgang*, even as Fogg had hoped.

As the Phantom crashed into him, they pitched backwards over the rail. The panorama of Paris whirled about him like a kaleidoscope. The Phantom grabbed at him as they fell, his lipless mouth twisted in a snarl. Fogg shoved him away and stretched out a hand, hoping he had calculated correctly. Pain flared through his palm and streaked down his arm as he caught hold of a truss and smashed into the side of the tower.

The Phantom fell away, a black blotch on the darkness, soon lost in the rain and wind. There was a rumble of thunder, and Fogg felt the Eiffel Tower shudder, as the Phantom's lair expired at last, somewhere far below the Champ de Mars. Muscles aching, body screaming for rest, Fogg clambered back up the side of the tower, towards the deck rail. When he at last grasped the rail, he was soaked through to the bone with rain and sweat, and his body was already convulsing slightly as the last dregs of strength left him.

He collapsed onto the deck, heedless of the rain that poured down on him. He needed time to rest. The anxieties and terrors he had experienced since the attack on Fogg Shaw Barrow had at last reached the point where he could no longer safely ignore them. So he lay there, soaked and trembling, his psychic boiler on the edge of bursting.

From time to time he twitched. His pupils dilated and contracted arrhythmically, and his lean frame shuddered with internal pressures that threatened to tear his mind apart from within. The rain continued to beat down as Fogg relived every terrifying moment, every negative emotion, he had experienced over the past several days.

When the thunder storm had at last passed, and the first orange streak of dawn was visible through the cracks in the gray clouds that still shrouded the sky, Fogg finally went limp and uncurled from the position he'd laid in for several hours. He was cold and wet, and was likely to take ill sooner, if not later. But he was alive.

Fogg dragged himself to his feet. His every muscle felt as if it were encased in lead, and his clothes were stiff with grime and damp. No one had yet become alerted to his presence on the tower, for which he was thankful. There was every chance that, while the Phantom might be gone, his men were still prowling the area. Not to mention Moran, whom Fogg was certain had survived, despite the best efforts of the Vampires.

It was while these thoughts ran through his newly purged mind that he noticed the absence of something. It took him a moment to realize Gurn's body was gone. A stain of sticky, rain-diluted blood marked where he'd fallen, but the youth himself had vanished. Fogg felt his hackles prickle. Had Gurn been there, as he suffered through his neural emissions, or had he already gone? Regardless, there was no telling whose side the young man was on, now, with his benefactor lost, and the organization he'd worked for in shambles. Fogg had no wish to find out, either. Weary, he began his descent. The war he'd been drafted into was done. Or, at least his part in it. Regardless, it was time to go home.

Below him, Paris awoke, and the shadows of night lifted.

At least, for the moment.

Epilogue

> Pemberley House
> Lambton
> Derbyshire
> November 1975

Violet,

You always send the best presents, Auntie. It took me more time than I care to admit, but the cipher is cracked, I admit, mostly thanks to the notes provided by Sir Beowulf before his untimely passing, and Farmer. The cipher was in the same language as the Savile Row papers, but polyalphabetic in nature—an Alberti cipher, if you can believe it. Very old fashioned, even for a man like the author. Then, knowing you, you already guessed that and have since read the attached manuscript. If you haven't, I suggest you do so now.

It should come as little surprise to you that Fogg's duel with the Opera Ghost was hardly the end of the matter. Real life rarely affords such tidy conclusions. From what I've so far translated from the second, I can safely say that Fogg did not return home to Derbyshire and Fogg Manor until the December of 1891. This was due, apparently, to his enforced involvement in a subsequent, though apparently unrelated affair in Ruritania, and then a further crisis which took him to Istanbul. I'm still working on those translations, so try not to let your impatience get the better of you this time.

Nonetheless, from what I can tell, a hasty exchange of telegrams and letters—sadly not included, as I would dearly love to have read those!—revealed to Fogg that his suspicions as to the fate of his wife, children, and manservant were all well-founded. Aouda Fogg had indeed made her escape, with her daughters, and had subsequently made her way to London, where she swiftly garnered the aid of a certain Baker Street consulting detective and apiarist of your acquaintance.

While Fogg apparently saw little value in either popular literature or celebrity detectives (I can hear your uncle rolling over in his grave from here), his wife was obviously of a different mind. She engaged the services of your uncle and set him on Moriarty's trail. By the end of that year, the man who had once been Captain Nemo was on the run.

Passepartout had escaped Moriarty's henchmen as well, though he remained in Derbyshire, in hiding, until Moriarty and his crew departed. Once they'd fled, Passepartout swiftly set about contacting the remaining Eridanean agents with whom he was still on friendly terms through coded messages passed via post and telegraph.

While Fogg had been content to let such bonds grow thin and frail out of what seems to be a misplaced desire to protect his family and friends, Passepartout was altogether more pragmatic. The Great Plan had failed, but that didn't mean there weren't others. Even as Fogg was fighting for his life in the catacombs beneath the Champ de Mars, Passepartout was alerting these men and women that Phileas Fogg had come out of retirement, however unwillingly. I'm quite certain that the result of these communications are included in the other, as-yet-untranslated journals, and likely explain Fogg's further adventures on the continent after leaving Paris.

Fogg seems to have kept his distance as Moriarty's illicit empire crumbled over the course of the next year, picked apart by enemies of all descriptions. There is some evidence that he faced off with Colonel Moran at least once more during this period, likely during the events in Istanbul I mentioned above.

By the way, those strange carvings Fogg found, in the hidden chamber of the barrow? The ones you sent the photos of? They correspond to similar markings found in Antarctica by the Pabodie Expedition of 1930, and to those found in Australia's Great Sandy Desert a year later, both of which my father paid some special attention to. You've read those journals I found at that Kensington flat during the Persano Affair, haven't you? And, of course, you were involved in that whole "Eye of Oran" debacle. It all paints quite an unpleasant picture.

The Eridaneans and their enemies the Capelleans weren't the first—or the last—alien species to make Earth their battleground. And just like them, those other expatriates are *still* here. Fogg knew. I think it was just as much a shock to him as it is to us.

The barrow is at the heart of things, or it's at least one small part of it. There's a reason that Fogg's adoptive father made Fogg Shaw his base of operations, though he apparently never shared it with his Eridanean comrades. Moriarty knew, I think. That'd certainly explain the undue strain the so-called Napoleon of Crime was under in 1889, according to Fogg's own words. Your uncle punched his ticket before he could make a play to use what he knew, for which we can be grateful, and the other fellows who took up the Moriarty name obviously never knew about it.

So many disparate threads, all running back to a single pattern—the sketches in Fogg's fifth journal, the Ruritanian affair in 1889, the strange device he took from Colonel Moran (and who was Tiger Jack working for then, I wonder—it certainly wasn't Moriarty!) after their confrontation beneath the Basilica Cistern in Istanbul in 1890, the events at Wardenclyffe Tower in 1903 involving the "Thoan," whatever that is, the disappearance of Harley Warren in 1924, the Finnegan Manuscript, all of the rest of it . . . it all ties together, Auntie.

Fogg figured it out, way back when. He put it all together, and then . . . something happened. The last third of the final journal is missing. The pages were cut out and taken. But I think I know where to find them.

Wish me luck, Auntie.

On the road again,
P.

About the Author

Josh Reynolds is a professional freelance author whose credits include novels, short fiction, and audio productions. As well as his own work, he has written for a number of popular media tie-in franchises, including Games Workshop's Warhammer Fantasy and Warhammer 40,000 lines. He can be found online at http://joshuamreynolds.wordpress.com.

Meteor House Titles

THE WORLDS OF PHILIP JOSÉ FARMER
Anthology Series edited by Michael Croteau

Volume 1: Protean Dimensions
Volume 2: Of Dust and Soul
Volume 3: Portraits of a Trickster
Volume 4: Voyages to Strange Days

WOLD NEWTON SERIES

Doc Savage: His Apocalyptic Life by Philip José Farmer

The Khokarsa Series
Exiles of Kho: A Tale of Lost Khokarsa by Christopher Paul Carey

The Pat Wildman Series
The Evil in Pemberley House by Philip José Farmer & Win Scott Eckert
The Scarlet Jaguar by Win Scott Eckert

The Phileas Fogg Series
Phileas Fogg and the War of Shadows by Josh Reynolds

SCIENCE FICTION ADVENTURE

The Abnormalities of Stringent Strange by Rhys Hughes

www.meteorhousepress.com

Lightning Source UK Ltd.
Milton Keynes UK
UKOW04f0318030714

234483UK00002B/15/P

9 780983 746164